THE LAST BITE

Apollonie Sbragia

THE LAST BITE

A Novel

Translated from French by Lynda Northwood

Original title: La dernière morsure

Cover: © by Lucile Gramusset

ISBN: 9798750657247

Legal deposits at the Bibliothèque nationale de France, the British Library, and the Library of Congress: December 2021

For my mother

Prologue

'Where exactly are you?'

'Just opposite the station in Nice. That's odd because I haven't been back there in ages. I think it must be more than ten years. It's a beautiful day. I wonder what I'm doing here… among these people coming and going without seeing me.'

Alex paused. Her gaze wandered to the large, uncurtained window overlooking the inner courtyard of the Haussmann building in Paris' 17th arrondissement where Docteur Levine saw her patients. An immense magnolia tree stood in the centre, bounded by a low stone wall covered with brown moss, the tree's fleshy green leaves lashed by raindrops.

Seven years had passed since the Masson case. And seven long years had not been enough to erase the investigation's scars. They had slowly taken over her mind the way creeping ivy wraps itself around a tree and chokes it to death. She had been in psychotherapy with Docteur Levine for several months because they had blighted her work.

After her latest slip-up—the one too many—Commissaire[1] Hervé had given her an ultimatum: psychotherapy or dismissal. And putting her work as a *flic*[2] on hold was unacceptable.

Alex put this alternative out of her mind and turned to Docteur Levine.

Docteur Levine watched and waited for her to continue recounting her dream. A pair of half-moon glasses sat on the tip of her nose; a slightly faded leather notebook rested on her lap in which she scribbled notes.

Alex knew very well that nothing escaped the therapist's notice. Neither her expressions nor her movements. She would be doing the same thing herself if she were questioning a suspect or witness: scrutinising the unspoken words and barely perceptible signs unleashed by the unconscious, better to betray the person you suspect is hiding something.

Docteur Levine nodded for her to continue.

'Yes, yes, I'm going to,' she thought, 'the clock's ticking, and Giancarlo's waiting for me.'

'All of a sudden, he appears in front of me on the pavement opposite. Even before I lay eyes on him, I can sense he's there. He's wearing his knee-length raincoat and scuffed Doc Martens…'

Her ears began to ring, paralysing her brain, compelling her to close her eyes with all her might. The full force of the seven-year-old memory engulfed her: the sound of Doc Martens in the hallway. Rhythmic steps, inexorably approaching. Scuffed Doc Martens: the only thing she could see tied up on her stomach when Masson entered the

---

1 Commissioner: UK equivalent rank is Superintendent.
2 French slang for a police officer; the UK equivalent is "cop" or "copper"

room. Alex shook her head to silence the sound of his heels clicking on the floor.

'Let's get it over with!' she urged herself.

Recounting her dreams was blowing on embers rather than ashes.

'He's holding his fists deep in his pockets. He's fiddling with something in the right-hand one…'

'What is it?' Docteur Levine asked interestedly.

Alex's eyes misted over. Her lips parted and then closed. Another question she would not be answering.

'He's watching me.'

Alex swallowed, her mouth becoming drier. She remembered that cold look, devoid of mercy, the prelude to barbarism.

'A car passes between us, an old Citroën AX. I follow it with my eyes. I'd like it to stop, but it turns at the end of the street… I look back. He's still there, standing in the same place on the pavement opposite. Suddenly, the crowd disperses, everything around us turns black. It's just him and me, facing each other.'

Alex clenched her sweaty hands and started rubbing her fingers together nervously, her eyes now darting back and forth.

Docteur Levine watched her without saying a word. Alex's fear was palpable and radiated from her.

Docteur Levine put her pencil down on her notebook and slowly removed the glasses from her nose. She looked into Alex's eyes and smiled. Alex clung to that gaze with the feverishness of a castaway clinging to a lifeline.

'His mouth stretches into a kind of smile.'

Alex rolled up her lips to reveal her teeth, imitating Masson's carnivorous smile. Her tongue unconsciously caressed her canines, extending the mimicry to the tips of her teeth. When she realised what she had just done, her face tensed. Masson sweated from her every pore, cold drops trickling between her shoulder blades.

'That's when I woke up,' she added laconically, not prepared to admit that she had woken up screaming, her insides wrenching with terror at the thought of him finding her.

Feeling this last confidence coming to her lips but unable to express it, Docteur Levine gave her another encouraging nod. But Alex was looking down at the Persian carpet under her feet, studying the golden arabesques.

'There is a new and unexpected element in this dream,' Docteur Levine announced.

The two women stared at each other, letting an opaque silence stretch between them.

'You didn't tell me what colour the car was?'

'Red,' said Alex, breaking her silence. 'What's unexpected?'

Docteur Levine gave Alex a penetrating look to emphasise the seriousness of her words.

'He's contaminating a past he has never been part of. He's contaminating the memories you have without him.'

And as she calmly put her glasses back on the tip of her nose, she concluded, 'I must insist we revisit what happened in that room seven years ago. Think about it, Mademoiselle Ramblay.'

When Alex left the building at 5 rue de Guersant, she immediately spotted Giancarlo's unmarked car waiting for her down the street. He was sat behind the wheel, engine off, head bent forward slightly. His two-metre height and broad build filled the passenger compartment. He wore a shabby leather jacket and his black hair had hardly been combed–a far cry from the "classy" Italian archetype. Born in Rome, moving to Paris aged thirteen, he had kept the accent and various expressions that sometimes escaped his lips.

Alex ran to the car to avoid getting soaked by the pouring rain and opened the driver's door. Giancarlo turned his head towards her, hardly surprised.

'We said I was driving today,' he complained in his gravelly voice.

'Giancarlo, I need to do it,' she insisted.

They looked at each other for a moment unblinkingly. Giancarlo seemed to be weighing the risk of letting Alex take the wheel when she "needed to do it". He clumsily extricated himself from the car after a moment's hesitation while she stepped aside to let him pass. He looked down at her, visibly annoyed, and she met his gaze with a teasing smile.

'I'll be careful, Giancarlo,' she promised to reassure him.

Giancarlo took a few strides around the car, cursing the rain, and got into the passenger seat as Alex took her place behind the steering wheel, slamming the door shut. He did not even have time to strap himself in before she roared off, her right foot crushing the accelerator pedal. The car sped away, splashing the pavement and a few outraged passers-by as she hit a large puddle. Giancarlo nervously buckled his seatbelt, cross with himself for having given in again, and gave her his darkest look, his thick eyebrows furrowed as if he were scolding his children.

Alex concentrated on driving the car through the narrow Grands Cavaliers streets, her mind and body tense, trying to put some distance between herself and the dreams that had stayed with her.

The journey continued without another word to the sound of the wiper blades rocking back and forth; it took them to 36 rue du Bastion[3].

---

3 Address of the Direction Régionale de Police Judiciaire (DRPJ), the criminal investigation division of the Police Nationale, and Paris police headquarters since July 2017

1.

'George, here!' the man shouted for the fifth time before stopping his run.

Out of breath, exhaling white mist in the early morning chill, he listened attentively, trying to locate his dog which had escaped and run headlong into the forest beside the lake.

He had made jogging along the lake before work a habit since adopting the beagle. It wasn't the first time that George had bounded off on his own through the woods in pursuit of a bird or a hare. Barely a year old, George was still being trained. He would sometimes ignore the heel command[4] and follow his natural hunting instincts instead.

The man could hear George's muffled barking a few yards away towards the lakeshore. Exasperated, hands-on-hips, he called the dog one last time before consulting his watch. Realising that this whole escapade was making him late, he, in turn, left the path to look for the beagle.

Just as he spotted his dog half-hidden by a bush, the barking gave way to a muffled growl: George had

---

4 The dog must work directly next to its master instead of behind or in front

managed to catch his prey and was busy mauling it.

The man leant forward as he walked towards his dog, squinting between the branches to see what George, frantically pulling on his hind legs, had hold of in his mouth.

It was not an animal.

Puzzled, the man quickened his pace, and in seconds had closed in on George, who was shaking his head furiously, his teeth sunk into the contents of a black plastic bag.

The bundle was about one metre long, wrapped in an ordinary bin bag that George had just torn open. Slowly, the man bent over his dog.

He gagged when he discovered what was in the bag, promptly turned around, and threw up his entire breakfast on his feet.

2.

Alex woke up to Nicolas Demorand's familiar voice on France Inter. Faintly crackling because she had never bothered to tune her radio alarm clock properly, but it did not matter. She turned it off with a gentle tap and lay in the warmth of the sheets a few minutes longer. She dawdled; she did the same every morning. It was invariably cold in her apartment—or else she slept badly. Each day, she had to summon up the courage to extricate herself from bed and set her feet on the cold tiles.

She didn't have time to run this morning because they had an early appointment with Commissaire Hervé. She had no idea why. The day before, Giancarlo had said to her with his customary casualness: *'Lascia perdere*[5], we'll soon see…'* He was probably right. She would run this evening and get a good night's sleep. Perhaps, at long last, without dreaming.

She wrapped herself in the bathrobe she lay on top of the duvet when she went to bed. She headed for the kitchen to make herself some coffee.

---

5 *Forget it*

She looked out of the window while the coffee machine was heating up. The dreary weather was never-ending. It would doubtless rain again today. And those heavy white clouds heralded more to come—snow perhaps, cold for sure.

She split open a brioche and began cutting it into small pieces. She then swallowed her coffee in one gulp and jumped in the shower. No make-up: she avoided mirrors. She pulled on a pair of jeans, rummaged in the wardrobe for a jumper and a mismatched pair of socks. Lastly, she slipped on her boots, pulled her black cap low over her eyes, and donned a pair of leather gloves.

Alex took one last look around her flat from the door-step as if unsure she would be back there that evening. She frowned as she realised that she had not touched the brioche, still in small pieces on the kitchen table. She left it, closed the door behind her, and ran down the stairs.

She lived on the fifth floor of an old building without a lift in the rue de l'Hermitage—a working-class district in the 18th arrondissement. She would not go in by motorbike today; it was bitterly cold, and the rain was already coming down in Paris.

Alex arrived late at the Bastion, her hair soaked and face reddened from the biting cold. She lingered in front of the large entrance, a rain-soaked tricolour hanging limply above it. She stepped inside and said a quick hello to some of her colleagues on the way to Commissaire Hervé's office.

The commissaire's office was located at the far end of the vast open-plan space on the third floor, reserved exclusively for the Crime Squad. The partition wall was entirely glazed and Alex slowed down to observe from a distance what was brewing in there. Commissaire Hervé was sat at his desk, not saying a word, his expression closed as usual. Giancarlo stood leaning against the wall with his hands shoved into his jeans pockets. A third person completed the picture, seated opposite the commissaire: a young man with short-cut hair, sat bolt upright in his chair. She could only see him from behind.

Thinking back in time, she saw herself in that same room seven years earlier. Sat in that same chair, facing Commissaire Hervé, Giancarlo to the right stood staring at her. It was the first time they had met. She had turned towards him. They locked eyes for a few long seconds. What she had sensed back then had been confirmed throughout their partnership. What he had thought of her back then, he had revealed to her as she lay in a hospital bed, stood by her bedside. They had just completed their very first team investigation: the Masson case.

Commissaire Hervé looked up as soon as Alex walked through the door. He sighed in exasperation, or with impatience, probably both. Giancarlo and the young man turned simultaneously. And as three pairs of eyes fell on her, she understood the purpose of the meeting. She said a quick hello and sat down on the vacant chair facing the commissaire. She turned to the young man on her left, and they stared at each other.

Alex examined his face in detail: thin, long, straight nose, thick lips, and dark eyes. The look was frank and direct. But, as serene as he came across, she recognised the nervousness in his pupils: he was probably a freshly trained officer.

She had two hunches. The first was that this young man

had not landed in the police force by chance but by true vocation; she had perceived raw and total commitment. The second unsettled her; was it because he hadn't given the scar around the corner of her mouth a second glance when most people openly stared? She would rather not think about it anymore and to cut it short, turned to Commissaire Hervé.

'Let me guess... A recruit from the Crime Squad, and he's for us!'

Alex forced herself to smile. Her relationship with Commissaire Hervé had not been going well lately—to put it mildly. Her recent misdemeanours had all too often brought her in here for lengthy reprimands.

'Lieutenant Diop comes from the 19th arrondissement. He has just completed his probationary period there. He worked for a year with Commandant[6] Ducret, who you know well. I encourage you to give him a call for that matter. He's the one who recommended him to your care,' said the commissaire, looking at Alex and Giancarlo in turn.

He handed Alex the file containing Lieutenant Malik Diop's service record. She grabbed it, opened it, and quickly read through the main points in front of the person concerned.

'Consider him a gift. His record is excellent,' added Commissaire Hervé.

Alex closed the folder and handed it over her shoulder to Giancarlo, who dived into it, squinting to accommodate his eyes. Giancarlo would read it in detail with his usual thoroughness. He would not fail to see Ducret again over coffee either, to dig into this new character they were

---

6 *Commander: UK equivalent rank is Chief Inspector*

obliged to welcome–with a certain reluctance–into their well-established duo.

Cutting off any possible comment, the commissaire said, 'Since you're here, we have just been notified about a child's body, found this morning on the banks of Lac d'Ailette. Two hours east of Paris.'

'Two hours from Paris? What the hell are we going to do there!' Giancarlo said, looking up from Malik Diop's file.

'The Parquet National[7] has taken up the case and mandated us. The local police district has said, and I quote, it is not competent to take charge of such a "sordid" crime,' explained Commissaire Hervé, aware that he had just piqued their curiosity with these last words.

'What do you mean?' asked Giancarlo.

The commissaire jotted down some information on a Post-it and handed it to him.

'The child's body has been mutilated,' he added. 'I'll leave you to find out more of the details for yourselves on site. You can thank me; you won't be too many trios on this investigation!'

---

7 Prosecutor's Office with the responsibility for prosecuting criminal cases and representing the interests of society in civil litigation.

THE LAST BITE

3.

The unmarked car had been monotonously racking up kilometres for more than an hour. Giancarlo had authoritatively taken the wheel without any protest from Alex. Malik had followed them in silence, which was a good start because Alex and Giancarlo were sparing with words and pointless conversation.

Alex was going over the latest information they had received from the commissaire: the local police had secured the area, the forensic team was already at the scene, the medical examiner was there too, all under orders to wait before moving the child's body.

The very fact that it was a child made Alex nervous. She had never worked on a case involving a minor. Glancing at Giancarlo, she wondered if, as a father, he felt the same way, but he was his usual focused self. She then looked in the rear-view mirror at Malik, who was staring straight ahead at the road, impenetrable. Alex was the last to leave Commissaire Hervé's office and had taken the opportunity to observe him: tall and lean, his walk lithe and graceful, the opposite of colossal Giancarlo, whose unyielding gait seemed to anchor each step in the ground.

What made her doubly nervous was that the child had been "mutilated". The very moment the commissaire said the word, a cold shiver ran down her spine. It had taken her several weeks of therapy, and as many particularly harrowing sessions, for the nightmares to subside. And all it took was a single word to bring back fear with the nauseating whiff of a seven-year-old past.

Alex suppressed these thoughts and looked out of the window at the steadily moving scenery to distract herself. The sky was low, grey, and heavy. Their car had left the hyper-urban Paris region and was now navigating through alternating meadows and fields in the Picardy countryside. Flocks of sheep enjoying their grazing despite the rain passed before her eyes, a few horses too. Mist stretched out in a smooth blanket into the distance.

Was it Malik's presence that made this mission special? She and Giancarlo knew each other inside out. They complemented each other; their routine was well-oiled. During their working relationship, reflexes had naturally become ingrained over time; each had their allocated roles and looks replaced words most of the time.

The more Alex brooded, the more stress built up inside her, causing a knot in her sternum.

The Lac d'Ailette road sign came into view. Giancarlo took the exit onto a quiet road; they drove along for another twenty minutes. Alex was sat back in her seat, taking in the scenery, when they saw flashing lights to their left some five hundred metres away.

They turned into the car park next to the lake. And as soon as Giancarlo switched off the engine, a young woman in uniform came trotting towards them.

'Capitaine Ranieri?' she asked as Giancarlo got out of

the car.

'Indeed,' he replied, noticing the young woman's reddened eyes, a clear sign that she had just been crying.

'Officer Philippes. We've been expecting you,' she added without hiding the relief in her voice. 'The medical examiner wants to dispose of the body as soon as possible.'

They followed her along a steep and narrow path that dipped down to the lakeshore. Alex and Giancarlo walked side by side, Malik walked behind, seemingly wanting them to forget him. Alex turned around and looked at him. She gave him a questioning nod; he nodded back that he was following. The ground was muddy, their feet sank softly into it, putting one foot in front of the other require more effort than usual. They could hear the familiar crime scene hum in the distance: popping photo flashes and raised voices.

At last, the lake appeared in front of them: a vast, dark, still surface stretching for several hundred metres, cloaked in wisps of grey mist. Surrounded by a dense forest of ancient trees and clumps of rushes, both perfectly reflected in the mirror-smooth water. The forest encroached on the lake in places, its trees bending dangerously towards the surface, lazily dipping their branch tips.

A footpath ran along the shore, dropping intermittently into the forest. A water sports centre and, as far as they could make out from where they stood, a restaurant with a terrace on stilts had been built on the shore facing them, deserted that day but probably packed out in spring and summer.

Then they saw the crowd of police uniforms and white suits. It was pretty obvious but not yet distinguishable that amidst this commotion was the child's body. Alex took the lead and pushed her way through the men and women busying themselves all around.

The child's body had been left carelessly on a carpet of mud and dead leaves, wrapped in a commonplace bin bag. The bag had been ripped and torn open, exposing the body from head to shoulder.

Alex covered her mouth with her hand.

All the noises around her became muffled before disappearing completely.

The arm had been severed from the body; the shoulder joint was cleaned out.

From the bundle's size and shape, it was easy to see that both legs and the other arm had been removed too, despite the bin bag covering it.

All that remained of the child was the head and torso.

4.

'Porca miseria[8],' said Giancarlo, seemingly himself.

Malik was pale, his jaw clenched. He stood back, silently taking in what he had just seen. Nevertheless, when Giancarlo turned to him, he held his gaze.

'Welcome to homicide,' the latter said to him glumly.

Malik would have to get used to putting distance between himself and corpses if he wanted to stay in the Crime Squad.

'In the twenty years I've been working in the division, I've never seen anything like this… Doing this to a kid!" Capitaine Labonté exclaimed from behind them—he had been overseeing operations until their arrival.

'How was the body discovered?' asked Giancarlo.

'A jogger, around seven o'clock this morning. His dog found it.'

'Has the body been identified? Is the kid local?'

Capitaine Labonté shook his head and said: 'I've sent two of my men off to carry out some door-to-door enquiries, but I'm rather pessimistic… There's nothing around

---

8 Holy shit

here within three or four kilometres; you can see that for yourself. It's the most deserted area of the lake. Compared to the other side, which is residential. It also has a leisure centre that gets quite busy, especially during school holidays. But here, at the beginning of November…'

A few more flashes popped before the camera fell silent. A man in a white coverall came to interrupt them: 'We've finished. We need to pack everything away and get back as fast as we can before the samples degenerate. Although I can tell you straight away, with the best will in the world, we found hardly anything…What with the mud, the dog, and the jogger, the ground was already completely contaminated by the time we got here.'

'When will we have the first results?' asked Giancarlo, handing the forensic technician his business card.

'Within 72 hours, maybe less… In any case, I will send you the photos later today,' concluded the technician, checking the business card in his gloved hand to make sure Giancarlo's email address was on it.

Then he left, making way for the medical examiner who was growing impatient behind him.

When Giancarlo's eyes fell on the medical examiner, he could not help but stare at her: she was petite, her hair in a big bun tied at the top of her head, her big black eyes hidden behind thick red tortoiseshell glasses. She clutched her briefcase firmly to her chest. She did not wait for Giancarlo to speak to her. As soon as they made eye contact, she started. She listed all the information she had been able to gather from the body and that she was able to divulge without getting too far ahead of herself like a metronome: 'The body is that of a white male child about ten years old. From the body's rigidity, temperature, and after taking the cold weather of the last few days into account, I would say that death occurred two or three days ago. All four limbs, upper and lower, have been severed. The cuts are clean. All the mutilations are post-mortem a priori. I would also say, but obviously the autopsy will confirm it, the probable cause of death was an incision made in the left temporal carotid artery.'

Giancarlo did not take his eyes off her and remained silent, hypnotised by the delicate mouth that had uttered these unvarnished details. Faced with his silence, which she interpreted as incomprehension, Docteur Saranches smiled awkwardly and felt obliged to add: 'His throat was slit, and he bled to death.'

She shrugged her shoulders as though to indicate there was no more to be said.

'I'm having him brought back to Paris. The autopsy will take place later today. Would you like to attend, Capitaine…?'

'Capitaine Ranieri. Yes. We'll be there.'

She nodded faintly, turned briskly on her heels, and headed for the car park. Giancarlo followed her with his eyes despite himself. She was only a few metres from her vehicle when she turned around, shaking her head—displeased with herself—and shouted at Giancarlo: 'I forgot! He has bite marks.'

And with her hand, she pointed to two places on her own body: the left cheek and the bottom of her right breast.

'The dog?' he asked, raising his voice.

She frowned and shook her head: it was not the dog.

Giancarlo nodded to confirm he had noted this last piece of information. The medical examiner turned and went on her way, leaning slightly forward because of the effort involved in lifting her feet from the mud with each step.

He then picked up the discussion with Capitaine Labonté where they had left off: 'Have you found the victim's limbs?'

'Not in this area.'

'The search area will have to be extended. The whole area around the lake needs searching.'

'Impossible, I don't have enough men! We're a small team. Nothing ever happens around here. I don't know how or why that body ended up here, but one thing's for sure, no one from here would be capable of such a horror,' the captain seethed, clenching his teeth.

Capitaine Labonté did not want to hear any more about this investigation, let alone take part in it, whether from afar or close by. He had done his job while waiting for the Crime Squad to arrive, and he now intended to wash his hands of it; this murder made him uncomfortable by its very nature and surpassed him by its sheer gravity.

'I'll see what I can do to get reinforcements,' Giancarlo conceded. 'In the meantime, I'm counting on you to do your utmost.'

Capitaine Labonté thanked him with a brief nod, followed by a curt salute, and left the site without a backward glance.

Giancarlo and Malik watched the stretcher carrying the child's body go past wrapped in an opaque plastic bag, followed by the local police leaving the crime scene behind their chief.

The two men found themselves alone, surrounded by silence and mist.

5.

Alex remained at the now-empty spot where the child's body had been discovered. She stood motionless, her hands deep in her pockets, examining the indentations in the muddy ground: dead leaves, a few twigs and small pebbles embedded in the sticky soil under the weight of the corpse abandoned there for several hours.

Giancarlo studied her as he approached. Her features were drawn, her face looked emaciated, she was exhaling a misty cloud from her half-open mouth. His eyes dropped to the scar encircling the corner of her mouth despite himself: a stippling of small whitish blisters. A scar he was careful not to lay eyes on in front of her.

Sensing the arrival of her two teammates, Alex turned towards them. She nodded to Giancarlo, who quickly summarised his exchanges with the different teams.

When he mentioned the bites, they exchanged a long look. Alex did not blink. She already knew because she had seen them on the child's body, where the garbage bag had been torn open by the dog.

This sudden tension between the two did not escape Malik. Without knowing all the details of the Masson case, he had been an indirect spectator, like millions of French people, seven years earlier. It had made an unprecedented impact on the media. As a lycée student at the time, he had followed it closely and ardently read all the information he could unearth, already fascinated by crime stories and what it took to be a detective.

Somewhat taken aback by the exchange of glances between Alex and Giancarlo, Malik realised that this new investigation had echoes of that old case. He remembered the picture on all the news websites' home pages. A clear shot of a young *flic*–Alex– being carried out of Masson's so-called lair. His arrest–which brought a series of murders of rare savagery and a hunt lasting several years to an end–had caused an unprecedented media frenzy. Journalists had no sense of decency. They broadcast this photo with Alex's face visible on the internet and social media. She was lying on a stretcher trolley pushed by two paramedics, her dirty hair clumped together in thick strands, her eyes half-closed, her gaze absent.

A tall man with a cigarette balanced on the corner of his mouth is in the same photo, dragging along a man in handcuffs, his head covered with a jacket. Uniformed officers surround them, leading the way to a police car. Malik learnt later–when he started his police career–that the man who had just laid hands on Masson was none other than the young woman's partner, Capitaine Ranieri.

In this photo, Giancarlo was stood stiff and brooding. He had just nailed the serial killer who had eluded the Crime Squad for more than three years. Until, that is, the Ramblay-Ranieri team's arrival on the case.

'The murderer tried to dispose of the body at the bottom of the lake,' she said. 'For some reason, they were interrupted. Look at that pile of large stones.'

Giancarlo and Malik turned mechanically to follow Alex's finger. It was clear from the imprints left on the child's body that the stones were not there by chance. The murderer was preparing to weigh the body down before making it disappear.

The three of them stood pensively in front of the lake, seeming to want to pierce its surface with a single glance and probe its depths.

Giancarlo took out his phone and dialled. As he waited for the prosecutor to pick up, he whispered to Alex: 'I'm asking for permission for the Brigade Nautique[9] to intervene.'

As Giancarlo fell into conversation with the person at the other end, Malik turned to Alex: 'You think there are others, don't you? Bodies... at the bottom of the lake.'

She nodded and saw in Malik's eyes what she was herself feeling at that very moment, what every police officer felt when a lead was taking shape: feverish and excited.

'Maybe I'm wrong...' Alex added, 'but I have a feeling that this isn't the first or the last... I think there'll be more. The bite marks on the face and chest...'

'Tomorrow,' cut in Giancarlo, who had just hung up, 'operations will begin at daybreak.'

After carefully putting his mobile phone away in the inside pocket of his leather jacket, Giancarlo approached the edge of the lakeshore and walked along a few metres. There was no pier on this side. There were no signs of a boat having been hauled out of the water. A few boats could be seen on the opposite shore by the marina and the

---

9 Underwater Search Unit

leisure centre.

'How about we go over there?' he suggested.

Giancarlo took one last look at the crime scene. When he turned to go, he saw Alex and Malik walking alongside each other back to the car park and talking. Giancarlo's eyes followed them, and a feeling welled up inside him that had been alien to him until then. He lengthened his stride to catch them up, and they headed off towards the marina.

Giancarlo drove slowly, taking in the neighbourhood. It was just as Capitaine Labonté had said: clean and middle-class. A tree hedge lined the road running alongside the lake for several kilometres, broken up by large gates: modern steel ones, others wooden, older-style and painted, or wrought-iron. These gates protected the entrance to mansions with pitched slate roofs, overlooking vast gardens or with direct access to the lake. As they approached the town centre, the landscape markedly changed. The road started to be punctuated by charming townhouses, often semi-detached, in alternating pastel colours reminiscent of North Sea coastal towns. The leisure centre was located on the town's edge, sprawled over several thousand square metres, with the main building, a well-organised constellation of small bungalows, and some well-placed tree-lined areas. The whole place was intensely quiet. They passed very few cars, just a few people walking about, accompanied by their dogs, or pulling shopping trolleys.

'The door-to-door investigation will have to extend to this side of the lake,' Malik said. 'All these houses have a direct view of the shore where they found the kid. We don't know what time the murderer dropped him off, but there's a good chance it was at night, and they used a torch to find their way around.'

Alex stared at Malik in the rear-view mirror. Admittedly, his remark was pertinent, but she was immediately struck by him referring to the victim as the "kid" and all the empathy he had put into that simple word. She was about to pick him up on it but held back at the last moment, gently biting her bottom lip. Why mother him? What was happening to him?

'That's a good point, Malik,' agreed Giancarlo. 'I'll ask them to go door-to-door on this side as soon as we get to the station. With a bit of luck, Labonté will have thought of it himself,' he added, turning to Alex with a look that spoke volumes about his opinion of the captain.

They parked in the marina car park, which was open and free of charge at this time of year. As they got out of the car, Giancarlo spoke to Malik as he readjusted the collar of his jacket: 'We're just doing a routine investigation. There's no need to mention the body, even though this kind of news travels fast. Let's try to find out if there was any night sailing in the last few days or if they have noticed any unusual activities. Our guy was probably waiting for a boat that never came...'

'Or it came, the person bringing the body was disturbed and had to leave in a hurry,' said Alex.

Giancarlo nodded and then turned to Malik: 'Should we let you conduct the interviews?'

Malik was taken aback at being thrust into the limelight so early into his new post. He looked at each of them in turn and nodded nervously.

Giancarlo pointed with his chin to the marina office.

There was no time to lose.

An hour later, they were back in the car and debriefed

on the way to the police station.

Sat in the back, Malik was consulting his notebook. He synthesised and summarised the information he had gathered, turning pages back and forth. Alex and Giancarlo listened to him, nodding regularly.

'The Lac d'Ailette port has three piers: one for the marina managed by the municipality and open to the public, a smaller one managed by a private sailing club in the town in collaboration with the Rotary Club, and a third managed by the leisure centre. There are three types of boats: motorboats, sailboats, and a few pedaloes. There's no security system, no surveillance cameras. However, all three piers have a night watchman.'

Malik paused and looked up at the road ahead as he took time to reflect before continuing adroitly: 'In short, whoever wants to can easily borrow or steal a boat... All trips are logged. The logs are computerised except for the municipal marina log. They log trips "the old-fashioned way" in a large notebook.'

Malik smiled to himself as he thought back to the weighty tome brandished proudly by the receptionist.

'No night-time activity. Too cold at this time of year. No unusual activity of note. We'll get the list of club members and records tomorrow.'

He closed his notebook with a sharp snap, sighed quietly and ran his hand over his head.

'Good job,' said Giancarlo as they reached the police station.

The grim raw concrete of the building perfectly matched the November greyness. They made their way towards the main entrance, already convinced that they would not learn much.

They could see that Capitaine Labonté had not lied: he was severely understaffed. The offices were cramped, and although you could safely assume that some officers were in the field, the size said it all about the headcount.

Capitaine Labonté gave them a frosty welcome, disappointed to see they had come back so quickly, and just as he was finishing with the jogger's statement.

Still upset, the runner had not given away anything vital to the investigation. He confirmed that he ran every morning at the same time along the lake with his dog. Shocked by the discovery of the child's limbless body, he had stumbled backwards and managed to drag the beagle back to the path by its collar, the dog pulling at its leash and barking at the corpse. He dropped his mobile phone several times before coming to his senses and calling for help. He did not move until the police arrived, a wait that seemed interminable, having to keep the beagle from going back to play with the bin bag. He did not see anyone at the scene, which was no surprise at this time of year.

The door-to-door investigation was still underway, but nobody had seen or heard anything so far. That was no surprise either since the first house was more than three kilometres from the crime scene.

While waiting for reinforcements, Capitaine Labonté had dispatched three of his officers to search for the victim's limbs in the surrounding woods. They would not be back before the end of the day. The whole operation would undoubtedly take several days because of the area that needed to be covered and the size of his team.

The captain huffed in exasperation when Giancarlo asked him to extend the door-to-door investigation to residents on the opposite side of the lake but gave in again to get rid of his Crime Squad colleagues. He bellowed an order to the last two officers still in the building, who stood up without hiding their lack of enthusiasm and conspicuously shuffled out.

Giancarlo thanked Capitaine Labonté, who did nothing to hide his relief, and they left with the feeling that the chances of getting anything out of his team were very slim.

It was nearly 1:00 p.m. when the three of them met up outside. The rain was coming down. The three walked on together in silence for a few minutes, having decided to have some lunch. Giancarlo had pulled up the collar of his jacket and was walking with his shoulders hunched against the rain. Alex pulled her cap down low over her eyes. As for Malik, he was moving forward nonchalantly, paying no heed to the raindrops falling on his head. He had regained his appetite—a sign that he was naturally disposed towards crime work as far as he was concerned—and was looking in all directions for a place to sit down and eat.

After wandering more than a kilometre, they came across a small restaurant, possibly the only one open in the area as it was packed. Once seated, Malik relaxed, reassured that he would soon have some food inside him. Giancarlo shook the rain out of his hair while Alex went over their conversation with Capitaine Labonté: 'It's most likely they dumped the body the night before as the jogger said he used the same path every morning at around the same time.'

'Hmm…' muttered Giancarlo, absorbed in the menu.

'When we get back to the Bastion, we'll have to search through the missing persons to identify the victim,' she said, turning to Malik. He rolled his eyes as though to say he was not devoid of experience and insight.

When their order arrived, Alex went back to thinking aloud: 'I don't know about you... but I don't think the crime happened here... For me, it's just a good place to dump the body.'

Giancarlo, who had thrown himself on his rib steak, looked up from his plate, the tension in Alex's voice palpable. He paused to look at her, his mouth still full. Alex had not touched her food. She was leaning on the table, her chin resting on her intertwined fingers, her gaze lost. Giancarlo could feel Alex's right leg twitching nervously under the table. She had been talking about nothing since they sat down, about things that did not need to be said, that did not need saying to each other after seven years of working together and were obvious, even to Malik, who was still a bit new. Giancarlo suspected what was bothering her were the bite marks. Echoes of the torture Masson had inflicted on her years before had brought memories to the surface. She was desperately trying to suppress them.

'Alex...'

He waited for her to turn towards him and looked into her eyes.

'Mangia un po' per favore,[10]' he pressed her gently, pushing her plate towards her.

He put his heavy hand on her leg to stop the twitching.

'Yes,' she conceded, her voice altered.

She slowly untangled her fingers and carefully picked up her fork. She played with the tomato slices and took a few bites here and there.

Gradually, the ambient hubbub—customer conversations, the clatter of cutlery, shouting orders to the kitchen—

---

10 Please, eat something

enclosed them in a bubble. They finished their meal in silence.

6.

They arrived well ahead of time at the Institut Médico-Légal[11] in Paris. They were told to wait in the waiting room that Malik was discovering for the first time. Stripped of all decoration, the walls bare and faded, it was strictly limited to the essentials: a few basic chairs, a cold drinks dispenser, and a coffee machine.

'"Scratched? Scratched how?" I asked the teacher,' said Giancarlo, becoming agitated, talking with his hands–a reminder of his Italian origins. 'Anyway, she answers me, she scratched her little classmate. Full stop. The problem, Monsieur Ranieri, is that it's not the first time.'

While recounting his interview with his youngest daughter's teacher, Giancarlo was crudely imitating her mannerisms.

'Does this also happen at home with her brothers? I answered, of course not! It's most likely because she's being bullied! My daughter's not going to let that happen, *no è il caso di scherzare*[12]!'

Then taking Alex by the shoulder, he brought his face

11 *Forensic Institute (IML)*
12 *No kidding!*

close to hers: 'Well Alex, you know Angelina! Can you imagine?'

'Yes, but Giancarlo, put yourself in the parents' shoes. How would you feel if Angelina was scratched by a classmate? Just be thankful they didn't press charges…'

Giancarlo continued: 'I'll skip the lecture she gave me… I'm an officer of the law… Blah, blah, blah…' he said, grimacing and brushing away what he considered to be a load of old tosh with his arm.

'So, what's next?'

'The girl was punished… And you know what?'

Grabbing Alex by the shoulder again, he fumed: 'She wants her to see a psychologist! For a few slight scratches! *Porca miseria[13]…* '

Alex nodded. Just as she opened her mouth to try and calm him down, they were interrupted by Docteur Saranches' assistant: the autopsy was about to begin.

They did not need to ask Malik if he wanted to attend the autopsy. That went without saying. He followed them in without a word, with his incredible ability, despite his size, to remain unnoticed. They felt the cold. They passed the rows of lockers filled with corpses and entered the autopsy room. Apart from the cold, it was the smell of putrefaction and death that hit them. Malik fought back the urge to vomit with a superhuman effort.

Docteur Saranches was waiting for them, dressed in a white lab coat, looking solemn behind her red tortoiseshell glasses, her hair pulled back into a tight bun. She stood at one end of the autopsy table with the child's dead body

13 Bloody hell

already laid out on it, her hands resting one on either side of the head. Her assistant was a young intern wearing thick glasses that distorted her eyes, making them look abnormally large, and made them feel uncomfortable.

As their eyes glided over the body, Giancarlo removed a small round jar from his inner pocket. When he removed the lid, the contents gave off a powerful smell, a mixture of camphor, cloves, and menthol. He took some of the balm on an index finger and slowly smeared a little under each nostril. He passed the jar to Malik, who had turned dangerously pale as his eyes came to rest –despite himself–on the mutilations that had left the boneless joints gaping and bare.

After giving the three police officers a moment to look, Docteur Saranches began the autopsy.

Malik was trying not to pass out. His mind began to float above him–a defence mechanism against the barbarity on view before his eyes. Switching to autopilot, he picked up his notebook and pen and began to write. Docteur Saranches' voice came to him muffled, mitigating the horror of the findings that came out of her mouth. More pictures, surgical blade incisions, sample taking. The room began to swim. He clung to his notebook as you might grip a life raft to keep from capsizing.

'I'll spare you the usual findings. I gave them to you this morning at the crime scene, and they'll be in my report,' Docteur Saranches began.

After measuring and weighing the body, Docteur Saranches started to examine it from the head down. First, she gently lifted the eyelids: 'Nothing special. Dark eyes, brown, I would say.'

She moved to the nose, armed with a small torch to

inspect the nasal cavities.

She gently curled back the lips to look at the teeth, and while tilting the corpse's head back, she said: 'I don't know if you noticed, but he has a diastema between the upper central incisors.'

She must have felt a wave of incomprehension run through the audience because she paused, looking at the three of them, and added: 'It's what we commonly refer to as lucky teeth.'

She opened the child's jaw wide. With gloved fingers, she proceeded to count out loud the milk teeth followed by the adult teeth.

'It's just as I told you before,' she said. 'He's ten years old, twelve at most. Based on the size of the trunk, he must have been between 1 metre 45 and 1 metre 50 tall.'

'The weight is a bit trickier. He lost a lot of blood. I would say about fifty kilos.'

She brought her face close to the body and scrutinised every inch of skin. With the help of her intern, she turned over the trunk, which they inspected together equally rigorously. Finally, they studied the genitals. They worked as if they were alone in the room, exchanging remarks, questioning each other, all the while using medical jargon that largely eluded the three police officers. Docteur Saranches straightened up from time to time to deliver her conclusions, trying to make them as straightforward as possible.

'Apart from the two bite marks on the face and right breast, there are no other signs of sexual violence. The genitals are intact. I took samples. The lividity indicates that the body has been moved. The victim didn't die at the crime scene.'

'The shape of the bites and their size at first glance...'

As she said this, Docteur Saranches paused and reached into her instruments for a flat steel ruler. She measured the size of the bites precisely.

'These are the bites of an adult. The jaw is medium-sized. I'm not sure what more we can tell from this…'

Momentarily pensive, Docteur Saranches stood holding her chin with her gloved hand, stained with organic matter, causing Malik to retch.

'Is it possible to make a cast?'

'We can indeed try, but the bites aren't deep. I'll have a go,' she said, waggling her finger at Alex. 'I'll also try taking a sample. There may be some matter left.'

'Saliva?'

'That's it…' Docteur Saranches muttered as she carefully ran a swab stick over each bite.

She finally inspected the head and neck, indicating the carotid artery incision that extended a good ten centimetres.

'As you can see, the incision is very clean, as are the incisions made to remove the four limbs. The object used was a knife with a sharp, non-serrated blade and large enough to do such precise work. Especially at the joints.'

Docteur Saranches stood up straight and continued: 'He died as a result of his external temporal carotid artery being severed. The dismemberments were post-mortem. But that's not all.'

Malik was still in a state of shock. It took a few seconds before he realised that Docteur Saranches was about to deliver a vital piece of information. He looked up and saw that all eyes were on him. He nodded slightly to indicate that he was ready for the next part.

'I made a note just before you arrived,' Docteur

Saranches explained as she moved to the back of the child's head.

'Come closer.'

They obediently joined Docteur Saranches. They bent together to get a close look at the top of the child's head—except for Malik, who had decided to spare himself further discomfort. They followed Docteur Saranches' gloved finger with their eyes. In the child's mud-stained brown hair, they could see dried blood clumped together. She pushed the strands of hair aside, and they could see the mark left by a blow and a bruise. They both stood up at the same time.

'Someone knocked him out before cutting his throat,' Giancarlo concluded.

'Indeed, the mark you see indicates that it was with a blunt object. I would say a bar, a log, a bat.'

Docteur Saranches delved more deeply into the hair strands and added: 'I don't see any residue… pieces of bark… A smooth object, I would say.'

Once all the external observations were complete, she grabbed an electric saw with a conviction that was puzzling for such a small woman. She cut open the thorax without further ado and rummaged around inside, removing, and weighing every organ, emptying what there was to empty. Alex and Giancarlo exchanged stupefied looks at this almost surreal scene.

'All the organs are in good condition, the liver slightly enlarged for a child of this age, but nothing abnormal. There was not much in the stomach at the time of death. We will proceed with toxicological analysis and send it to you as soon as we can.'

Giancarlo opened his mouth to speak, but before any

words came out Docteur Saranches added: 'Allow two to three days for the autopsy report.'

And while Alex and Giancarlo shared their findings with Docteur Saranches, the intern cleaned up the body, sewed up the large T-shaped incisions in the chest before thoroughly hosing down the zinc table and tiled floor.

Hearing the squeak of the wheels, Malik turned to follow the intern pushing the cart towards the anonymous morgue lockers.

And after more than an hour of suffering these final outrages, the child finally found peace in the cold darkness of locker number 12.

THE LAST BITE

7.

It was Alex who drove them back to Le Bastion. Unusually for her, she went slowly. It had been a long and exhausting day.

Malik sat in the back, typing up and saving all the notes he had taken during the day.

Giancarlo took the opportunity to go home to his wife and children.

Alex walked home in the dark and rain amidst the bustle and the looming Paris lights. She stopped at the grocery shop on the corner of her street and bought the few things Michel had asked her to get for him. She would drop them round later in the evening. Once home, she changed quickly out of her work clothes, put on her trainers, and ran back down the stairs. The damp cold outside hit her. She set off across the cobblestones towards the Seine quays, weaving in and out of people hurrying by. She accelerated. She needed to bring up all the bile that had built up in her over the last few hours.

This overload flashed through her mind in jerky images: their arrival at Lac d'Ailette lake, the mist, the child's mutilated body, the purplish bites on his alabaster skin,

popping flashbulbs, Malik looking back at her in the commissaire's office, the sound of the saw cutting into the
thorax, Malik's dazed look in the autopsy room, weighing
the liver, emptying the stomach, Giancarlo's rib steak, her
fork that weighed three tonnes, the bitumen gliding under
the car's wheels.

She lengthened her stride to run faster and faster again
to clear her thoughts. She concentrated on her breathing,
sucking in the stinging cold air and exhaling to the end of
her breath. The images gradually faded until all she could
hear was the muffled sound of her feet on the cobblestones, her steady breathing, and her heart beating.

It was a little after 10:00 p.m. when she arrived at
Michel's house. Michel lived a few blocks away from her in
a sixth-floor flat without a lift. He didn't go out anymore. It
was Alex who did his shopping for him.

She knocked vigorously on the front door.

'Michel, it's Alex! It's me!' she shouted, knocking again.

She put her ear to the door, recognising the sound of
the TV set and, eventually, Michel's heavy, slow footsteps
approaching in the hallway. She stepped back as she
heard the key click first to unlock the front door, then the
two extra locks. The door opened a few inches. Michel's
suspicious eye peered at her through the crack for a moment before he undid the chain and opened the door
wide.

Michel greeted her with the usual: 'Ah, it's you! Come
in, come in.'

He smiled at her and tenderly patted her cheek. Exactly
twice.

Michel was monochrome, dressed in a shade of brown.

Weighed down by his seventy-three years, he preceded her down the corridor to the living room where a large flat-screen TV was blaring. It created a disconcerting anachronism with the rest of the decor frozen in the eighties. He sat down and waited for Alex.

Alex closed the door behind her, turned the keys in the three locks and put back the chain. She took off her hat, gloves, and jacket and hung them on the coat hook on the back of the front door. She went into the kitchen and put away the groceries she had bought earlier in the Formica cabinets. She washed her hands and wiped them on the old tea towel hanging by the sink.

She stood there for a moment, contemplating this space suspended in time.

Michel had withdrawn from life's daily tasks since his retirement. He spent his days enclosed in his flat in a solitude punctuated by TV programmes and Alex's visits.

She joined him and sat on the floor at his feet, her legs crossed under her.

He put his hand on her head, patting it gently: 'Was it a hard day?'

She nodded.

And that is how they stayed: immersed in the latest twists and turns of a Detective Murdoch investigation.

THE LAST BITE

8.

Alex slept very poorly: the bad dreams were back. To ward off the recurring nightmares, she strayed from her habit and took a long look at herself in the mirror: pupils dilated, nose straight, nostrils quivering, lips pale and dry, and finally, the scar encircling the corner of her mouth. It had been seven years; the wounds had healed, but not her head.

She dressed quickly and went to the kitchen. The brioche she had dutifully taken out of its wrapper while preparing her breakfast was still intact. It sat there—as it did every morning—with an air of reproach.

It was another day without hunger[14].

She heard a short blast of a horn in the street. Giancarlo was getting impatient. She glanced at the alarm clock… 5:08 a.m. They had a rendezvous at 5:00 a.m. sharp. She ran down the stairs and suddenly found herself in the biting early morning cold. She quickly got into the waiting car, double-parked right outside her front door.

14 *Reference to Delphine de Vigan's Jours Sans Faim (Days Without Hunger, 2001) written under the pseudonym Lou Delvig*

'*Ciao Bella*,'[15] Giancarlo said, his face still bore the marks of too short a night.

'*Ciao Bello*,'[16] Alex retorted, fastening her seat belt.

And so, he drove off. Only when sat back up in her seat did she notice Malik in the back. Habits die hard. For seven years, it had been just her and Giancarlo.

On any other day, she would have turned around and started a conversation: 'How are you doing, Malik? Did you make any progress last night?'

But today was a day without hunger.

They drove in silence for almost two hours until they found themselves back beside Lac d' Ailette. Each of them wondering what its depths held in store for them beneath its seemingly calm and innocuous surface.

Capitaine Labonté welcomed them as amicably as he had left them the day before. The Brigade Aquatique teams were already on site. They could see a ten-metre-long zodiac in the distance along with a larger boat with tapered white hull: the latter was equipped with a sonar to locate any suspicious masses on the lake bottom. Three divers were getting ready onboard the lighter boat. Indeed, Alex spotted one already in the water, a few metres away from the zodiac.

All they could do was wait.

Giancarlo took the opportunity to enquire about the results of the search entrusted to Capitaine Labonté. Unsurprisingly, Labonté advised that the child's limbs were still missing and that the door-to-door investigation had produced no results either. Giancarlo thanked the Capitaine

15 *Hello beautiful*
16 *Hello handsome*

for all his efforts—not without a touch of irony—and approached the lake to better monitor the Brigade Aquatique, which had just gone into action. He mechanically looked for his cigarette packet in the inside pocket of his jacket. As he sighed in frustration, he met Alex's amused look.

'Ah, that makes you laugh!'

She smiled, exhaling white wisps into the cold early morning air. Then, turning to Malik, she explained: 'He quit smoking last year and is still looking for his fags…'

They walked along the lake where the shore was passable, keeping an eye on the underwater operation's progress. From time to time, they could hear Capitaine Labonté's walkie-talkie crackle. They turned and looked at him. Invariably, the Capitaine would nod his head, a gesture he accompanied with a desolate expression.

It was almost midday when Alex realised that the divers would not find anything. Her intuition was still telling her that this was not an isolated murder. She stood alone for a moment, motionless, scanning the lake with an aftertaste of unfinished business.

The rain began to fall in large drops, transforming the lake surface into vibrant lace.

'You see, I've got a SIG Sauer Pro SP2340,' Giancarlo commented as he pulled his weapon from its holster.

'For me,' he said, placing his hand flat on his chest, 'this is the most reliable and accurate weapon. I've had it since I joined the police.'

He nodded and added: 'Senti,[17] it's used mainly in the

17 Listen

USA by American Drug Enforcement units. It's a bit heavier than the 2022, which is what we use here but... *no lo so*[18]... it sits nicely in the hand.'

Malik drew his gun in turn. He cocked it, then disarmed it.

Giancarlo looked at his face and saw a hint of pride.

Malik pondered, seeming to weigh the words.

'It's a 2022, not that we got given a choice... It does the job,' he said with a shrug.

Giancarlo looked at Malik solemnly, reminded that this was a young recruit eager to learn, eager for peer recognition.

'We'll do a training session together, and you can try mine if you like,' he added.

Malik smiled, his face relaxed.

'Capitaine Ranieri!' shouted Capitaine Labonté as he trotted towards them.

Alex, Giancarlo, and Malik swung around together, eager to hear what he had to say. Capitaine Labonté stopped dead in front of them. They understood immediately from his expression what he was about to tell them.

'The divers found nothing. They're packing up.'

Barely able to contain his joy at being rid of this investigation for good, the Capitaine shook hands with the three officers in turn and walked away, leaving them in a silence heavy with disappointment.

When they reached the car, Giancarlo said to Malik: 'For the firearms session, Alex will come along too, because if there's someone who can teach you anything in this area, it's her! She's an outstanding shot!'

18 *I don't know*

9.

Back at the Bastion, they went straight down to the self-service for lunch. The three charged into the large dining hall, to be greeted by the cleaner mopping the floor and looking rather annoyed. The chairs had been upturned onto the tables to make cleaning easier, except for one where two of their Drugs Squad colleagues sat talking. They exchanged a few words.

Once they were in front of the self-service display, eagerly and hungrily eyeing what was left, Danny came out of the kitchen to serve them. Well-liked by all the Bastion *flics*, Danny was always smiling and joking with everyone about anything and everything. He had been working in the kitchen for more than twenty years. Everyone knew his story: Danny did not hide the fact that his son had Down's syndrome. He was happy to share the difficulties he encountered with specialist institutions and rejection by society in general.

Once served, they sat down and ate in silence, Malik watching Giancarlo watching Alex and trying to make sure she was eating properly. Surprised by his concerned look, Alex slowly put her fork in her mouth and chewed conspicuously. Giancarlo shrugged his shoulders and began to eat the way he always did, devouring his food as if he had not eaten in days, nose in his plate.

Once they were full, their tongues loosened, and they talked about everything and nothing. Alex and Giancarlo questioned Malik about his life in the suburbs. He remained evasive, briefly mentioning journeys out in the morning and back in the evening on the dirty, overcrowded RER D[19]. He didn't say anything about the difficulties of becoming a *flic* in this microcosm that detested them. On the other hand, when Giancarlo asked him about his experience with Commandant Ducret, Malik was all talk. Alex and Giancarlo were unsurprised to learn that he had been able to take part as an officer in training in the epilogue of dismantling the Hodja brothers' prostitution ring—the case was relatively recent and had created a lot of noise in the media. The complex and multifaceted network had spread its tentacles into all strata of Parisian society, from underworld to upper crust, including the guardians of the republic: the police, political, and legal bodies. Ducret and his teams often lost their nerve. Several times they found themselves on the verge of giving up. They finally won the game by arresting some thirty people—including several high-profile public figures—with which Malik had been able to help. He told stories about the outcome with enthusiasm, which confirmed Alex's intuition that Malik had joined the police out of vocation.

But when Alex asked him what had motivated his request for a transfer to the Crime Squad after such a rewarding collaboration with Ducret, Malik clammed up and

19 *Réseau Express Régional or Regional Express Network. RER D crosses Paris from north to south.*

became evasive: he was young and wanted to see other things was all he would say.

Alex went to collect the photos she had sent to the print centre. She caught up with Giancarlo and Malik in the office that Commissaire Hervé had allocated to them for the duration of the investigation, located at the bottom of the corridor on the third floor.

She put up two photos of the victim in situ on the wheeled evidence board, left a space and marked up some key information. She spread the rest of the photos on the round table in the centre of the room: shots of the corpse taken from different angles, along with close-ups of the bites, and the hollowed-out joints. The child's hairless face lay frozen in death with his eyes closed, chapped and purplish lips, and the mark left by a blow to the back of the skull.

Alex moved to the back of the room, leaned against the wall, and contemplated the result from a distance: it was thin gruel.

She remembered how she and Giancarlo had been enlisted in the Masson case investigation room seven years earlier. They were called in as reinforcements when the investigation had been stalled for three years. The first thing they had discovered was an overstretched and disillusioned team, and then not one but three evidence boards filled from top to bottom with photos of the victims.

Malik turned to Alex, pointing to the small space on the board deliberately left empty, and asked: 'What's this for?'

'The child's photo when we have identified him,' she replied laconically.

Alex and Malik each sat down at computers and began

searching the central police missing person databases. Giancarlo stood to one side by the window to call the public prosecutor and give him a full report on the situation.

Giancarlo could hear the familiar sounds of children playing in the apartment as he approached the front door. Jerky little footsteps running in all directions, laughter, and screaming. He opened the door slowly and saw Angelina in her pyjamas coming out of her room dragging her "Mister Frog" blanket, worn out from repeated cuddling. She ran clumsily into the kitchen, and he could hear her moaning to her mother. He didn't pay any attention to what she was saying, he knew Angelina's unceasing recriminations about her older brother by heart. He always felt a touch of tenderness when he heard his wife's calm and gentle voice, trying to dampen her daughter's fury. Without being in the room, he could guess the caressing looks his wife gave the little girl. As he took off his jacket and put his gun out of the children's reach, Giancarlo let the warmth of his apartment envelop him. He relaxed and made his way to the kitchen, the nerve centre of the household at this time of day. He saw Angelina and Mister Frog appear: 'Daddy! Marco came into my room, and he kissed my blanket! It's all dirrrrrrty!' she complained, stretching out the first syllable.

Giancarlo took his daughter in his arms and slapped a loud kiss on her cheek.

'How was your day at school, *cuore mio*[20]?'

Angelina shrugged her shoulders like a grown-up: 'Daddy, I'm hungry. Can I have a sweet?'

_____

20 *Dear heart*

Giancarlo put her down without answering and let her run back to her room. He leaned against the doorframe and watched as his wife filled the bottom of a tart with vegetables. When she finally looked up at him, she gave him a weary smile. She put the tart in the oven. Wiping her hands with the cloth tied around her hips as an apron, she approached her husband to kiss him on the lips.

'We can eat in half an hour. I got home a bit late.'

She sighed, forced herself to smile again and added: 'I'm tired… and they're overexcited tonight! Let's eat and put them to bed early. It won't hurt them. Would you read them their story after dinner?'

He nodded. Easing past him, she announced: 'I'm going to put my pyjamas on too!'

He was about to follow her when the two boys burst out of the room shouting: 'Mummy! Mummy! Mummy! Marco broke my castle!'

'It's not true. It wasn't me! Nasty little sneak!'

Giancarlo intercepted them, grabbing each by an arm, and led them back to their room. Tonight, he would have to be patient again.

THE LAST BITE

10.

Giancarlo arrived at the Bastion at around 9:00 a.m., pleased to be back in the "club" atmosphere once more: the corridor conversations, halfway up the grand central stairway too, a small cup of coffee habitually in his hand; the comings and goings between offices; the people under arrest sat along the corridors, often looking distraught, sometimes insolent, always nervous. He immersed himself in the maelstrom by greeting a few colleagues. His face relaxed. He was able to put that morning's turbulence out of his mind—he had charge of the children and took them to school on Thursdays. He made for the coffee machine and headed to their office, espresso in hand.

Alex and Malik were already there, sat next to each other in front of several open files spread out on the table.

'*Ciao* guys, anything new?'

Alex was so engrossed that it took a few seconds for Giancarlo's words to sink in. When she finally looked up, she seemed surprised to see him there.

'Not really. I'm working on the missing persons with Malik. The forensics report is here. I'll let you read it, but there's not much. A usable boot imprint. We're talking about one person, a man with a small foot, size 40…'

While listening to Alex, Giancarlo grabbed the report from the table and immediately dived into it.

'However, there is still no autopsy report or results of the toxicology analysis,' she added.

Giancarlo decoded the message: they would have to start again and put pressure on the medical examiner. He got up straight away and went to the corner of the room to make a call to the Paris Institut Médico-Légal and Docteur Saranches.

'We'll have them by the end of the day,' Giancarlo announced as he sat down to go through the forensic report.

Alex and Malik divided between them the files that needed checking to identify the victim, each working on a separate computer.

As she looked through the missing person photos, Alex was already starting to think about the family. They would need to be notified, invited to the morgue to identify the body. She would need to escort them down the corridor to the cold room. She knew that the closer they got to the door, the slower their steps would be. She also knew that she would pretend to ignore their reluctance and firmly encourage them through it once it opened. And despite their strong urge to delay the inevitable, when the hope of seeing their child alive again would no longer be permitted, they would go in. This fragile hope would then turn into a fervent prayer, coursing through their veins to their very core like venom. The body would already be laid out on a table. Once the awful truth was before their eyes, distress would follow a brief and cruel hesitation. Anyone who has seen somebody they know lying dead will have noticed that uncanny and infirm distortion of their face abandoned by life, which provokes this overwhelming dissonance: it is them without being them.

At the very thought, her stomach contracted. Alex had been in homicide for over fifteen years now. It was not her first identification. She had taken part in identifying all the bodies in the Masson case bar none. She closed her eyes, and her finger froze on the mouse wheel. She felt terrible, but she could not help thinking that the added difficulty this time was that the victim was a child, as if, in short, a woman did not carry a lot of weight, as if on reaching adulthood we were nobody's child, as if by growing up we lose our sacred innocence, like a shedding skin replaced with a veil of impurity, which makes the desecration of body and soul more acceptable.

Alex forced herself to evade these thoughts that were swelling like a wineskin ready to press against the walls of her skull. She opened her eyes to see Malik openly watching her. She stared back at him until he gave way and dived back into his research.

The only sounds were those of Alex and Malik's mice, clicking, scrolling, and navigating through the missing person files, looking intently at the faces of missing boys. Page after page, photo after photo, many were class photos, taken at primary school or secondary school for the older children. The pose was invariably the same, a compulsory picture: the child stood slightly in profile looking towards the camera and openly smiling. You almost forgot that you were looking for a child whose throat had been slit, butchered, then wrapped in an ordinary bin bag and left in the mud.

A loud shriek broke Alex and Malik's concentration.

They both turned towards Giancarlo, now slowly opening his desk drawer. He rummaged around and finally pulled out a small black pouch. He removed a pair of glasses and placed them discreetly on his nose.

Ignoring the looks on the faces of his two teammates, he dived back into the forensic report. He could see for himself that the elements of the report gave them nothing to go on. The black bin bag used was a large chain store brand, widely available across France. The few fibres found on the body were from a synthetic material commonly used in the low-cost textile industry. No fingerprints, even partial ones, had been taken. Last, the DNA found was none other than that of the victim himself.

'A boot print...' scoffed Giancarlo as he tossed the report onto the desk in front of him.

Then Malik suddenly sat up in his chair and announced: 'I think I've got him.'

Alex and Giancarlo came up behind him and leaned over his shoulder to take a closer look at the photo he had just stopped on.

The corpse in locker 12 came back to life before their eyes thanks to the colour photo of a young boy with bright eyes, brown hair falling in curls over his forehead, full cheeks, and a shy smile revealing happy teeth. It took them a moment to correlate this real, living child with the chalky, lifeless one in the photo pinned to the evidence board. But there was no doubt in their minds: this was indeed a photo of the victim.

Giancarlo read out the missing persons notice issued by

the Police Judiciaire[21], his gravelly accent echoing around the room: 'Gabriel Jaumart. Age: 11 years old. Height: 1m48. Build: slim. Eyes: brown. Hair: short, curly, and brown. Ethnic group: European. Distinguishing feature: happy teeth. Clothing: blue jeans, red long-sleeved polo shirt with coloured stripes, black Nike trainers with fluorescent green laces, and a thin black down jacket. Disappeared: Wednesday 17 October at around 4:00 p.m. on his way to basketball practice—he never got there. The last person to see him alive was his mother. She had been at home that day and saw him leave the house at 4:00 p.m. as usual. For any information or evidence that would be useful to the investigation, contact the Service Régional de la Police Judiciaire (SRPJ) on 01 72 99 35 97.

Alex turned to Giancarlo, and they exchanged a knowing look: they were making progress. Giancarlo asked Malik to have the photo printed, sat back down at his desk, and called the number indicated to advise that they had found little Gabriel.

The still-warm print of Gabriel's photo was pinned to the evidence board, right next to the ones of the corpse that had just lost its anonymity.

The SRPJ captain in charge of Gabriel's disappearance insisted on accompanying the mother to the Institut Médico-Légal. He stayed with her to the end.

Gabriel lived alone with his mother. She was a nurse at Pitié-Salpêtrière[22]. She worked in the intensive care unit on

---

21 Judicial Police (PJ) responsible for handling penal law enforcement and investigation of laws and felonies under the direction and supervision of the judiciary.
22 A Sorbonne University teaching hospital in the 13th arrondissement

nights, which enabled her to take full care of her son when he came home from school. Gabriel did not know his father. He had never seen him, nor had he been legally recognised by him.

Gabriel had just entered the sixth grade. He had been walking to school alone since the beginning of the academic year. He was an unproblematic child, serious and diligent at school. He had played basketball from the age of eight at the Domremy Basket 13 club, a fifteen-minute walk from his house. He went there twice a week: on Wednesday afternoons from 4:30 p.m. to 6:00 p.m. and Friday evenings from 6:00 p.m. to 7:30 p.m. He always took the same route, passing along rue de Patay and then rue Jeanne d'Arc, as far as number 74.

Unsurprisingly, the investigation into Gabriel's disappearance had stalled.

Nevertheless, the police had found a witness. A regular at the "Aux Quatre Vents" brasserie on Gabriel's route. Unemployed for more than three years, Pierrot lived on income support and spent his days sat in the same place at the small table on the brasserie terrace next to the door. Here, he could quietly distract himself with the counter discussions inside. He could watch passers-by at his leisure, gloat over the altercations that broke out in the street between motorists, and watch Gabriel go by every Wednesday, between 4:10 p.m. and 4:15 p.m. to be precise, on his way to basketball practice.

Pierrot told the police officers who questioned him the day after Gabriel's disappearance that he had seen a woman of about fifty approach the child. He had seen them talking together for a short time, maybe ten minutes—hard to say for sure when you have several grams of alcohol in your bloodstream. He also mentioned that the child had seemed worried. The woman put her arm around his shoulders, and they had both started walking away. By this time, Pierrot had been distracted by voices coming from inside "Aux Quatre Vents", and had stopped caring about Gabriel, more absorbed in the swearing coming from the brasserie.

Pierrot was unable to describe the woman. "In her fifties and clean" was essentially all they had managed to get out of him. Of course, Pierrot was essentially a drunk. Continually mired in the mists of alcohol, he found it difficult to express himself clearly. His statement had been regarded with "great caution"; it was given no serious consideration at all.

The police had found no other witnesses. Gabriel's disappearance had been treated with complete indifference. It seemed just as easy to disappear on a busy city boulevard as on a deserted country road.

The police had thought Gabriel had run away to find his biological father. They had tracked him down to the south of France: he lived in Marseille and worked as a docker. But Gabriel had not come to see his father.

Very familiar with the internet and social networks, his mother closely supervised Gabriel's access to them. He had no personal computer, no tablet, and no smartphone. He had to rely on his mother's computer, and his access to it was limited to a few hours per week: Wednesdays and weekends. He mainly used it to play games or watch the latest videos from his favourite YouTubers. All the devices had been thoroughly analysed by forensic computer engineers searching for a sexual predator without success.

The first question Gabriel's mother had asked when she

arrived at the morgue was if her son had suffered. It was explained to her that he had not. His mutilations were post-mortem. He had been knocked out, and from that point on, it had been over very quickly.

The second question was when he had died. She began to weep as she was told, her frail and exhausted body racked momentarily with sobs. Holding back her despair, she asked in a daze what had happened to her son during the thirty long days between the day he disappeared and the day he was killed.

To this last question, they did not have an answer.

11.

'Let's contact Office Central[23],' suggested Giancarlo. 'Let's ask the Salvac[24] team to help us look for similar crimes in their database.'

'Maybe he's not a serial killer,' Malik interjected.

'That's true,' Alex admitted, 'but the bite marks on the…'

'You never know,' Giancarlo cut in. 'It's a lead like any other that we have to explore. And besides, we don't have much else to go on for the moment.'

He turned the pages of the toxicology report he had called Docteur Saranches for when the other two were at the morgue identifying Gabriel.

Sliding the report across to Alex, he summarised: 'Nothing in the blood… The triglyceride level is a little high… Nothing in the stomach.'

Giancarlo watched Alex scan the report for a moment, trying to catch her eye, and then added: 'She also drew a blank on the bites. Not enough matter, the samples were unusable.'

Alex pulled a chair to her and sat down at the table without taking her eyes off the toxicology report. She returned to the first page, which she dutifully smoothed with her hand and leaned over it, her head in her hands.

After studying each page in great detail, she concluded that they were indeed at a standstill. A knot began to form in the pit of her stomach.

Alex was the first to leave the locker room. The combat training room was empty. Few officers ordinarily used it and even fewer at this particular time of day. Still, it took her a few seconds to adjust to the rancid smell of sweat hanging in the air due to poor ventilation.

There was no boxing ring here, just a floor covered with blue and red Tatami mats. The red Tatamis were arranged in four by four-metre squares to mark out the combat zones. She placed her personal belongings against the wall and put on her gloves. When she looked up, Malik was walking towards her. She couldn't help but let out a whistle of admiration.

'I didn't know I was dealing with a French boxing pro! What class, Malik!' she said, eyeing him up and down.

Malik wore a red lycra bodysuit with white side stripes. The sleeveless suit moulded his body from shoulder to buttocks, revealing an athletic musculature. Malik advanced towards her, looking directly into her eyes. When he stopped, centimetres away, looking her up and down from his full height, she slowly raised her head towards him, evaluating the size of her opponent.

Keeping a straight face, Malik pounded his fist into his hand and asked her in a provocative tone: 'Good, can we start?'

Alex nodded, and they took their places opposite each other on the red Tatami mats while putting on their protective helmets.

Alex seemed to hesitate as she placed her mouthguard in her mouth and said: 'You don't have to go easy on me, OK?'

Malik, who already had his in, mumbled something that she did not understand. Irritated, he shook his head as if to say, 'Come on!' She then rang an imaginary bell, which she accompanied with a childish "ding-dong". And the fight began.

They instantly put up their guards and spun around each other, light on their feet, as Alex launched the hostilities. Malik was big and powerful, but she felt he was holding back; he was playing defence, using piston-action kicks to push her back and make her catch her breath. He would need provoking if he were going to forget who he was up against. And this she did admirably.

Alex had started learning French boxing in PE classes at school, which she had not enjoyed until then. She did not give up afterwards, continuing in clubs. She was soon spotted and started fighting competitively at the age of sixteen.

Alex threw a left jab at Malik, who tightened his guard to protect his face. Without waiting, Alex threw a front piston-action kick at his head that he did not see coming and took it full force. The look that Malik gave her—surprised, his pride stung—was unequivocal: she had hit the bull's eye.

The response was not long in coming. Malik delivered a head-level backhand that swept through her guard, followed by a lightning-fast right hook that hit her square on the chin and sent her to the mat, half stunned. If she did not lose consciousness, it was thanks to the protective helmet. And she stayed on the Tatami mat, breathless.

Malik bent down towards her, concerned.

'I went a bit too far...' he said, hampered by the mouthguard.

She looked up at him and held out her hand for him to help her up.

'One more round to go...' she muttered.

She banged her fists together as she hopped in front of him to prove she had come to her senses.

And she rang the imaginary bell.

The fight was over. The pair recovered alongside each other, breathing heavily, both lying flat on their backs, their legs up against the wall. Their feet were almost touching.

'You've got a hell of a spring. You're used to fighting people bigger than you,' Malik said.

Alex smiled and turned to him, suddenly serious: 'Why did you want to become a *flic*?'

He stared at her, taken aback by this almost intimate question: 'I don't know... It got to me when I was a kid. A certain fascination with crime, solving puzzles, I suppose. Why?'

'Well, you're from 91[25]... You don't have much time for *flics* when you're from 91, do you?'

Malik shrugged his shoulders.

'You... You mean guys like me, blacks?'

'No, I mean suburban kids... Don't put words into my mouth. There's a singer I love. A poet more than a singer

25 *French department known as Essonne in the Ile de France region.*

in fact, who said during a concert…'

Alex looked up at the ceiling, trying to remember the exact words.

'The suburbs are a double punishment: misery and ugliness.[26]'

As she said this, Alex turned her head and caught Malik staring at her. His gaze shifted from her eyes to her mouth. And she knew he was examining the irregular, slightly swollen scar that ran from the philtrum in her upper lip, around the corner of her mouth and back under her lower lip.

'Will you tell me one day how you solved the Masson case?'

Alex nodded slowly and looked away. She slid her legs to one side and stood up. Without saying another word, she headed for the locker room, leaving Malik alone and bewildered.

26 Abd Al Malik's Albert Camus, L'Art de la Révolte (Albert Camus, The Art of Revolt, 2016)

THE LAST BITE

12.

'I can feel that she's tired... She's got no patience with the kids, and when I come home, I get the impression she's avoiding me... She puts on her pyjamas and reads... I, like an idiot, watch TV...'

'Trouble at work?'

Giancarlo shrugged his shoulders and continued.

'Still, as you know,' he said, looking hard at Alex, seeking her approval, 'I'm doing my best to get home early these days!'

He shook his head and heaved a sigh.

'I come home; I look after the children... Well, it's true, at the moment they're not easy... Angelina is more and more awkward, and the boys... are boys... bickering, always looking for a fight.'

He sighed again.

'Shit, I'm tired too!'

'Talk to your wife, Giancarlo. Take some time together. Your mum could come over and babysit them for a night, couldn't she? Go to a restaurant, a movie. In short, time for you, without the kids...'

Alex smiled awkwardly and added: 'Well, I say that... I

don't know much about it...'

Alex and Giancarlo exchanged a long look. Alex had never really had a serious relationship, as Giancarlo knew very well. And since the Masson affair, it had been a wild-goose chase. Alex could not stand her body. So, how could she offer it to anyone else? She envied Giancarlo's home. It was not perfect but is there such a thing? At least there was warmth and noise when he came home. Her solitude weighed heavily on her. No one was waiting for her, and the place next to her in her bed was cold and empty. She straightened up and leaned back in the chair to put a stop to this uncharacteristic self-pity.

Alex and Giancarlo were waiting for Hadrien in the OC-RVP lobby in Nanterre.

Hadrien was one of seven agents in the Salvac team skilled and trained in using the eponymous software. Artificial intelligence software, based on complex mathematical algorithms and the ingestion of large volumes of data. It was capable of learning from the past and determining correlations and similarities between new and old crimes.

All crimes—solved or not—and so-called "worrying" disappearances up to 2009 were entered into its database. And thanks to an automatic data retrieval system, all new cases entered on the criminal police systems by any police officer anywhere in France were systematically recopied.

Salvac emanated from several experiments conducted in Canada, where serial killer numbers had increased over the last twenty years. It proved so successful there that it was exported, eventually, to most of Europe.

Hadrien finally arrived in the waiting room. He still had that slightly awkward, clumsy walk. Hadrien was the archetypal *no-lifer*: a brilliant computer scientist by day and an insatiable nocturnal *gamer*. His face bore the marks of all those nights spent playing online: his complexion was pallid, his eyelids droopy, and it was plain to see he lacked a balanced diet. He was not very tall, fat without being fat, and wore his long frizzy hair tied back in a ponytail. Alex had always seen him dressed in jeans and a t-shirt, as he was again that day. He was wearing a black Megadeth[27] logo t-shirt sporting a disturbing skeleton head announcing prophetically, *"This is the countdown to extinction"*.

'It's funny to see you with a mug in your hand. What are you drinking?'

'Green tea. Coffee made me too anxious. So, I stopped,' Hadrien replied knowledgeably.

Alex and Giancarlo exchanged a smile and followed him to his desk. Like the mug of steaming green tea, it did not match the person to whom it belonged: it was clean and tidy. The small items he kept on it consisted of a stack of three or four files, a few pencils, a fluorescent yellow highlighter, and a mouse mat. But what interested Alex and Giancarlo on this tidy desk that day was the hardware: two large flat screens next to each other. The left-hand one displayed the Salvac graphic interface, the right-hand one the contents of an investigation report. Hadrien had been kept busy since the formation of this research unit.

Hadrien borrowed a third chair and rolled it as best he could towards his desk. The three of them sat down, Alex and Giancarlo beside him. Giancarlo put Gabriel's file in front of him, prepared with Malik's help, in which they had listed the case characteristics in summary form. Hadrien opened it and took control of Salvac. He brought his

---

27 *One of the four big US thrash metal bands*

keyboard closer and grabbed the mouse. He closed the previous investigation on the screen, and the graphic interface disappeared before their eyes, leaving it blank.

Alex looked down for a few seconds, unexpectedly nervous. What if they didn't find anything? To calm herself, she concentrated on the keyboard sounds and the clicks of the mouse that Hadrien was skilfully manipulating. She looked up again and watched him. He felt her gaze and explained: 'I enter all the information, places, dates, names, facts without questioning. It can all be put to good use, correlated. We'll see what Salvac digs up, and then we'll play with the data.'

Alex nodded, intrigued by Hadrien's confidence in the software.

As he reached the details of the crime, he stopped short.

'Your case is truly gross…'

And they discussed with Hadrien the details of Gabriel's murder so that he could translate their investigative vocabulary for Salvac as accurately as possible.

Finally, Hadrien launched the search. He leaned back in his chair, took his mug, slurped, and began drumming his fingers nervously on the desk. Alex and Giancarlo remained motionless, their eyes on the small hourglass, a sign that Salvac was searching, calculating, correlating.

Suddenly, the software projected the results of its algorithms onto the screen. More than twenty cases appeared plotted in a graphic resembling a multi-limbed octopus whose body was the Gabriel case.

Hadrien brought up the similarities between the different cases and the graphic spread across the screen in a constellation of information bubbles. As he manipulated it, the octopus seemed to come to life before their eyes: pivoting on itself, changing shape, sometimes extending a limb, sometimes retracting one, its cerebral cortex stimulated electrically.

'Unsurprisingly,' Hadrien explained, 'we can see here that Salvac has brought up cases matching your investigation's discriminating features: child around ten years old, white, at least one mutilation to upper or lower limbs, single-parent family... But wait, there's more...' He approached the screen and quickly opened all the octopus' limbs. 'Mother in all cases... the victims are all from Paris Intramuros... a priori no relationship between the victims, none of them lived in the same neighbourhood or went to the same school.'

Hadrien paused and waited calmly for Giancarlo to finish scribbling in his notebook. When Giancarlo looked up, Hadrien continued: 'Let's get to the good stuff...'

Alex and Giancarlo exchanged a look of both surprise and excitement, this first list of cases revealed by Salvac was already a lot of information for them, much more than they had expected. They turned to the screen on the right, where a map of France suddenly appeared with pinheads in two different colours: red and blue. He zoomed into Paris and the surrounding area.

Hadrien studied it for a few minutes. Then, with a satisfied smile, he leaned back in his seat and bounced his legs nervously.

'The blue pinheads represent the places where the victims disappeared, the red pinheads...'

'... the places where they were found,' finished Alex.

Giancarlo squinted and decided to leave vanity to one side. He removed the small black glasses case from his inside pocket. Alex watched incredulously as he handled the brand-new glasses with great care and put them on his nose. She would have to get used to this Giancarlo version 2.0.

When he could finally read the map, his eyes widened in amazement at the results produced by artificial intelligence in a few short minutes. Without Salvac, they would have had to mobilise several men for several months to process this much data, with no guarantee of a result.

'Can you print all this out for us, Hadrien?' asked Giancarlo.

'Yep… but that's not all. I'm going to try one more thing.'

Hadrien leaned over his desk again. A few quick clicks brought up a brand-new graphic. He sat back in his chair, and the anxious leg bouncing resumed.

Alex and Giancarlo moved closer to him, trying to understand what had just happened on the screen that had triggered such excitement in Hadrien. They recognised a time axis, stretching between the first case in June 2013 and the date of Gabriel's murder a few days earlier. Between the two, some fifteen cases had been selected by Salvac.

'If we leave out 2015, your guy is following a pretty precise timetable,' remarked Hadrien.

Alex and Giancarlo were analysing the time axis and beginning to understand that two sequences were juxtaposed: the dates of the abductions and the presumed dates of the crimes.

When Hadrien added: 'Did you see that? He takes them in pairs. He kidnaps two kids two weeks apart. He holds them for a month and then gets rid of them.'

'… a fortnight apart,' continued Alex.

'And then nothing for several months before starting again,' Hadrien finished.

The three of them fell back in their chairs and remained there momentarily in a strange state of torpor. They each felt a mixture of amazement, relief at having discovered a modus operandi, and concern at the change in this investigation's magnitude in a matter of clicks.

Everything seemed to fit together disturbingly perfectly.

Alex contemplated this macabre chart, wondering why the murderer was abducting and killing two children in the space of a fortnight when something else struck her and instantly made her stomach churn.

'If all these crimes are indeed linked, and if this sequence is proven…' she said, waving her finger at the screen, 'it would mean,' and she turned to Giancarlo to look him straight in the eye, 'that there was a child abducted fifteen days after Gabriel and…'

Giancarlo's face froze as he understood what Alex was getting at. She swallowed hard and finished her thought: '… we only have nine days left to find them alive.'

As the penny dropped, the excitement abruptly dissipated. A nine-day countdown had begun in their minds. They had nine days to save the life of a child whose identity they did not know, being held somewhere in Paris by someone who wore a size 40 shoe.

And Hadrien, without waiting to be asked, questioned Salvac about the worrying disappearances in early November.

After meticulously checking the worrying disappearances selected by Salvac, it was past 7:00 p.m. when they finally reached a consensus on the most consistent. Hadrien printed out the precious charts, along with the summary sheets of all the cases potentially linked to Gabriel.

Hadrien accompanied Alex and Giancarlo to the OC-RVP exit and wished them good luck–without irony. After putting his already hissing headphones back on his ears, the prophetic Megadeth t-shirt wearer turned away and walked into the night with his distinctive gait.

Alex and Giancarlo exchanged a long look, a mixture of jubilation and apprehension.

Jubilation because they were convinced that they had taken a giant step forward and, that over and above solving Gabriel's murder, they could save a child's life.

Apprehension because they were aware of the difficulty of their mission. There was a plot, but it was still the result of a computer programme. And artificial intelligence software was not synonymous with truth or infallibility.

They were heading for the car when freezing rain started to fall. Alex ran and threw herself on the driver's door.

'Non funziona così[28], Alex!' growled Giancarlo, quickening his pace.

But pretending not to hear, Alex's face lit up with a smile as she opened the door to get behind the wheel. Giancarlo, still muttering in his beard, came and sat down defeated in the passenger seat, thinking that it had been a long time since he had seen that smile.

---

28 It doesn't work like that

13.

'Oh, it's you! Come in, come in,' insisted Michel. He looked at Alex for a moment, then turned his back on her and slowly walked down the corridor to the kitchen.

'I've brought your groceries, Michel.'

'Yes, I can see, pet! Why do you think I'm going into the kitchen, eh? I know I'm getting old, but still... look... put that down there,' he said, pointing to the small Formica table.

'Don't you want me to put them in the top cupboard?'

'No, no, we're going to eat, aren't we... you're going to eat with me, right?'

'I'm not very hungry, Michel, we came back late from Office Central. I've only just finished my run. You know, I have to wait a bit before eating.'

At these words, Michel stared at her for a long moment.

'Ah... but... come now, you're not just going to sit and watch me eat, are you?' he insisted as he moved closer to her.

He patted her cheek tenderly.

'You're not exactly fat now, are you?'

'A little soup then.'

'It's full of minerals. That's good after a run, isn't it?' he asked her with a wink.

Without a word, Michel emptied a carton of soup into a saucepan, put it on the stove to heat up and set the table.

Seated opposite each other, they ate amid the metallic clatter of cutlery and slurping of hot soup.

'So, you went to Nanterre today,' he said suddenly.

Alex raised her head, surprised that he had initiated a conversation about her investigation. Usually, when she mentioned her work, he showed little interest, often side-stepping this sort of conversation to talk about more mundane matters.

'Yes, the software they use is impressive. All that data, centralised and accessible, its processing power, making connections in such a short time.'

Michel stared at her for a long moment, the pupils of his eyes dilated.

'And little Pauline, do you think she's in this software?'

So that was it. Alex shook her head slowly.

'At the moment, the data only goes back to 2009,' she said.

'Hmm,' muttered Michel, taking another spoonful of soup. 'Don't get fixated on this serial killer assumption.'

'I know, but it's the only lead we've got at the minute.'

Michel nodded as Alex surreptitiously watched him, her eyes moving from the plate to his fingers, slightly damaged by the onset of arthritis. Michel had become drab: his eyes were dull, his skin loosened, his hair sparse and white. Far from the Michel she had known when she joined the police force.

'Say, I've received a letter from EDF[29]. I don't understand what they want from me. Can you look at it before you leave, pet?'

Alex nodded. They finished supper in silence.

Alex went home. Since they left OCRVP, she had been trying to concentrate on the grain of hope rooted inside her, being able to save a child. She forced herself not to think about what was happening to them in the hands of a torturer, a painful echo of her own experience seven years earlier. She clung to little Gabriel's autopsy, chanting over and over in her mind that he was not abused. If she wanted to stay the course, she needed to ignore this issue and concentrate on the outcome she wanted more than anything: to save the child before it was too late.

Before it was too late... Was Giancarlo too late seven years ago?

'Yes, he was too late,' she thought. Giancarlo had saved her life, in the strictest sense of the word. But by the time he had pulled her out of that filthy room, her soul had already been lost, trampled underfoot. A tear gently rolled down her cheek, which she angrily wiped away with the back of her hand. It was time to pull herself together and keep her inner strength to carry out this investigation.

And with this final thought, she fell asleep. But as she drifted off, she felt the sharp claws of Masson memories. He was there, lurking in the back of her mind, slowly creeping towards her. As sleep numbed her and weakened the barriers that she put up all day, he was gradually scraping and tearing away at the veils of her unconscious, greedily

29 *Électricité de France - electricity utility company*

engulfing it, and violating her dreams.

14.

As Alex walked down the corridor to their office, she spotted Malik in with the Vice Squad, deep in conversation with Stéphane. She approached and knocked on the open door.

'Hey, you're not stealing him, are you? We've only just got him on loan!' she said with a knowing smile.

Stéphane and Malik interrupted their conversation to say hello. She took the opportunity to step into the room and join them for a moment. Stéphane had been in the same year as Alex, but he still looked like a big teenager. His unruly hair had a rebellious lock that constantly hung over his eyes, and he was invariably wearing jeans and Converse sneakers. Yet, beneath this unkempt appearance lay an extremely competent workaholic.

'So how did it go yesterday?' she asked, addressing them both at the same time.

Malik had been enlisted the day before by the Vice Squad. They wanted him to lend a hand in a case centring around Les Pyramides, a neighbourhood close to Ris-Orangis in the Paris suburbs. Malik had lived there since forever. Les Pyramides was one of his old stamping grounds and where he had kept up valuable contacts despite his profession. When Stéphane had come to him for information about the wanted offenders named in the victim's statement, he had immediately understood that Malik's presence during the intervention would be vital.

'We managed to arrest three of the seven the girl reported to us. They're in custody for the moment. We're leaving them to stew for a bit before we resume questioning,' explained Stéphane.

'If you need a hand, don't hesitate to ask. I'll be in the bottom office,' Malik added.

They left Stéphane to join Giancarlo, already busy leaning over the worktable in the middle of the room. Malik had not been with them at the OCRVP and had some catching up to do. So, he quickly got rid of his jacket and dived into reading the documents laid out by Giancarlo.

'Start with this one,' Giancarlo suggested. 'Here, you see a summary of the cases most consistent with ours. There's a colour code for unsolved crimes and another one for worrying disappearances.'

Malik nodded at every word Giancarlo said. He regretted not having seen Salvac in action. Even though he was looking at what this software could produce for the first time, he understood the codes immediately.

He was looking at eighteen unsolved crimes and five worrying disappearances. Of the eighteen crimes, thirteen involved boys; the last ten involved using a bin bag; in only three cases—the final three—were there any bite marks. A sign of escalation or intensity, depending on your point of view.

Alex and Giancarlo finally showed him the last two charts that had caused such excitement: two maps, one showing the locations where the children had disappeared in red, and the other where their bodies were found in blue. Malik quickly saw that the disappearances had taken place in the Paris area, and the bodies were found within a one-hundred-kilometre radius. Either buried, sunk to the bottom of a lake or, latterly, dumped in a river. It confirmed Alex's intuition that, in Gabriel's case, the criminal had been interrupted before being able to sink the dismembered child's body to the bottom of the lake.

'Not too close, not too far... Always in different areas and consequently different police districts,' muttered Malik. 'He must be banking on the lack of inter-district cooperation. When local police find a body on their patch, they're unlikely to go looking for similar crimes in another jurisdiction unless they're particularly zealous investigators! And the case is soon forgotten.'

Finally, Giancarlo slipped the time axis under Malik's nose. They let him digest this last element. Malik methodically described aloud what he was looking at and what he understood. The time axis started in June 2013. He noted that you could see the sequence of victim disappearances and presumed deaths. He said nothing for a few minutes, taking time to study the series of events set before him. When he raised his head, he caught Alex and Giancarlo's insistent gaze. He continued his analysis aloud: 'In pairs? One child and a second a fortnight later... But I imagine not all the bodies have necessarily been found yet, so they're not listed in Salvac...'

'That's one possibility,' confirmed Giancarlo. 'The other possibility is that none of these murders is linked. Just the result of a mathematical correlation of a few discriminating factors... In any event, Salvac has revealed to us a modus operandi that requires confirmation. And for that, we need to study all these cases,' he concluded, laying his hand flat on the summary sheets spread out on the table.

Shaking the graph he still held in his hand, Malik added, 'but if Salvac is right, it would mean that...' he paused, looking from Giancarlo to Alex, 'even today, there's a kidnapped child somewhere, and we have...' he looked again at the graph and counted silently, '8 days to find them.'

The words hung in the air as if Malik had just passed a sentence that suddenly made the deadline real. Alex and Giancarlo nodded slowly.

'And this child would be one of these disappearances,' he said, putting his hand flat on the pile of worrying disappearances he and Hadrien had selected.

'Yes, these are the disappearances that fit the victim profile, our murderer's hunting ground, and took place a fortnight after Gabriel's kidnapping,' confirmed Alex.

Malik had deduced correctly. He backed away from the table and moved towards the window where he stood pensively, his gaze lost in the bustle on the boulevard below: indifferent passers-by hurrying along, cars stuck in traffic.

'What I don't understand is that we didn't find any traces of abuse in Gabriel's home. So... why does he keep them alive for a month before killing them?'

'No idea,' Giancarlo replied with a shrug.

'And in 2015, nothing?'

Alex pouted. 2015 was indeed a complete vacuum. There were no unsolved crimes or disappearances that matched their investigation.

'Either there are bodies still to be found—which is entirely possible—or our killer stopped for some reason,' said Alex. 'Perhaps illness, an arrest?'

Malik nodded. Did it all add up? The thread was tenuous. They were making progress, but they still needed to validate the preliminary hypotheses delivered by artificial intelligence. So many questions remained unanswered.

'What do we do now?'

'The priority is to substantiate and validate the Salvac findings,' Giancarlo explained. 'Perhaps look for bodies from 2015… Our murderer seems organised. So, why not in his choice of locations for concealing the bodies?'

'Eight days, Giancarlo,' reminded Alex. 'At the same time, we must start searching for the next victim.'

The three of them set to work, moving back and forth between the table spread with Salvac printouts and their computers, researching the various cases in more detail: investigation, autopsy, toxicology reports, and interviews.

Alex oversaw the board. She pinned the most relevant photos and clues on one side and listed outstanding questions and tasks down the other.

2015 remained a mystery. The three worked on the map to identify bodies of water where the killer might have disposed of the bodies. They would need a strong case to get the public prosecutor to agree to a substantial investigation, and a map from an unreputed software programme would not suffice.

They were still debating the validity of the Salvac results when Stéphane walked into their office. The interrogation of the Les Pyramides shooting suspect was about to begin. Stéphane had come to enlist Malik again.

Malik followed him, leaving Alex and Giancarlo to their animated discussion. Giancarlo wanted to wait until they had more evidence before asking the prosecutor. Alex was insisting that they should go straight away as time was short. When Malik found himself in the corridor on Sté-phane's heels, he could still hear their voices. Stéphane seemed completely indifferent to the arguing as if it were an all-too-familiar occurrence for the Paris Police Judi-ciaire.

When Malik entered Stéphane's office, he immediately noticed the suspect arrested the day before sitting on a chair with a laid-back and irreverent attitude. Malik knew full well what to expect from him now: an unpalatable mix-ture of primitive machismo and insults about black treach-ery. The objective was not to change the mentality of the man they were about to interrogate. It was just to get his confession and the names of his accomplices, using the man's language, which Malik spoke only too well.

Across the corridor, Alex and Giancarlo were still staring at each other when Giancarlo decided to cut short their dis-agreement. He put his glasses back on his nose and en-grossed himself in the open file in front of him. Alex's eyes went from his closed face to her own hands, still shaking with anger. She shrugged and walked out of the office to get away from him: his attitude had become unbearable.

Alex momentarily wandered about in the corridor be-fore she headed for Stéphane's office. She could hear snatches of the interrogation more clearly as she got closer. She recognised Malik's firm and steady voice. She also heard another voice, insolent and rude, which she im-mediately identified as the rapist's: 'The girl, she was there playing the slut. From the first evening, she had her legs spread. What does it say to you, I tell you!'

'Yes, what does it say?'

'She's a bitch, a slag! Wait, we tell her: "Come on, let's

go to the cellar, quiet-like." The girl follows you... she knows what's going to happen, you're not going into a cellar to show it off! I don't know. You don't go into a cellar for a look-see...' he added, shrugging his shoulders.

Alex approached discreetly and leaned against the doorframe to listen to the rest. The rapist had his back to her. She could see Stéphane facing her, sat behind his desk simultaneously typing up the statement and conducting the interrogation. Malik was sat on the corner of the desk, leaning on his leg slightly towards the suspect, creating a certain intimacy, as if this was a quiet chat among friends. The suspect, however, was beginning to show some signs of irritation. He was feeling, despite himself, that his arrogance and pride were overtaking the defiance he needed to keep up towards the police to have a hope of getting out of custody quickly.

'And once in the cellar, what happened?'

'She got what she was looking for, the slag, she got screwed!'

Alex's stomach instantly twisted at his last words. She clenched her jaw and met Malik's eyes. He understood in a flash what was about to happen and straightened up in a state of alert. But he didn't have time to open his mouth to intervene.

'She was willing, I'm telling you... Oh, and it's OK, we didn't have to burn the bitch either, although that's what she deserved!'

Alex rushed at the rapist with the speed of a wild animal at its prey, filled with hatred and fury.

Malik saw them both fall to the ground with a loud crash and the chair hurled violently to one side. The suspect found himself on his back, his eyes bulging, completely stunned by the ambush.

Sitting on the rapist's chest, Alex immobilised his arms with her knees, crushing them with all her strength on the ground. With her left hand, she pinned his head down, and with her right, she strangled him by compressing both carotid arteries. Alex was squeezing them so hard that her knuckles had turned white while the rapist, his eyes rolling back, was turning dangerously red.

Coming to his senses, Malik gestured to his colleague to stay put. He moved behind Alex and straddled the downed suspect's body. Pressing himself firmly against her back, he wrapped his arms around her. Alex's body was tense, her muscles hard as a rock: she would hold on until he was dead. He covered Alex's hands with his own and began to loosen her grip on the suspect's throat, whispering in her ear.

'Alex… It's OK… I've got it… Alex… It's OK.'

Touched by Malik's reassuring words and breathing in her ear, Alex slowly came to her senses. Her body gradually relaxed until she let go completely. They stood up together as the suspect still on the ground curled up on his side and tried to catch his breath.

Alex looked around in a daze to see Stéphane looking dumbfounded.

What had just happened?

Giancarlo was leaning against the wall by the way into the open space, absent-mindedly chewing on a toothpick. He was both far enough away not to be noticed and close enough to be able to peer into Commissaire Hervé's office, which is where Alex was. She had her back to him and was sat bolt upright in her chair despite the dressing-down she was getting from the commissaire. Commissaire Hervé was facing her. Having been in the same situation himself before, Giancarlo recognised the cold, angry expression that tightened his face.

The commissaire was still talking to Alex, his lips tight, when suddenly he threw himself back in his chair and raised his arms to the sky in a theatrical gesture of exasperation. Giancarlo was familiar with this gesture; his father used to make it when he was a child, muttering: "*E come fare un buco nel acqua*[30]".

Commissaire Hervé fell silent and stared at Alex for a long moment. Was she defending herself, Giancarlo wondered? From behind, she seemed to have been struck dumb. After what seemed like an eternity, Alex finally stood up. He saw her place her gun and police badge on the commissaire's desk. She left quietly, closing the door behind her.

With bated breath, Giancarlo stood up and scanned Alex's expression, trying to guess the severity of the punishment.

She walked over to him and delivered the verdict in a flat voice: 'Ten-day suspension and the shrink twice a week!'

'Alex, do you want to talk about it?'

'No, I'm out of here,' she replied grimly.

Giancarlo tried to hold her back, but his hand clutched air.

She descended the central staircase and left the Bastion by the main door without so much as a backward glance.

---

30 It's as much good as making a hole in the water

THE LAST BITE

15.

Giancarlo and Malik were sat next to each other in front of the evidence board. It now had an enlarged map pinned to it on which they had recorded the main features of the places where the victims had either disappeared or been found. Just below was an enlarged chronological sequence pinned with the victims' photos: those of them still alive above the date they disappeared and those of their bodies above the presumed date of death. This juxtaposition of life and death made the chronological sequence unrelenting and oppressive.

Malik had also drawn a big question mark in red marker pen on top of the presumed date of the most recent abduction: fifteen days after Gabriel's, according to the modus operandi that went back as far as 2013 according to Salvac's calculations. The very sight of this superimposed question mark accentuated the urgency of identifying the next victim. His gaze shifted to the right-hand side of the board where Alex had lined up the photos of children who had disappeared around that date: Antoine, Nicolas, Chloe, David, Julie. The string of lost children.

Malik took his head in his hands and tried to

concentrate. They had both been stood silently staring at the board for an hour, unable to decide what to do next: search for the 2015 bodies or find the next victim.

Giancarlo stared at the door to their office, his arms crossed over his chest. He imagined Alex walking through it, raging, urging him to contact the public prosecutor immediately, and scolding him for having procrastinated too long when it was the only sensible thing to do. He would have given in to her stubborn but welcome insistence because Alex always knew what needed doing. Carried by the strength of her convictions, she never had any doubts. He and Malik had been bogged down in the Salvac calculations' validity and veracity since the morning. The results spread out before their eyes gave them consistency and legitimacy... but were perhaps too good to be true.

Giancarlo sighed and rose heavily from his chair. Alex was not coming. His frame slowly unfolded, lifting him out of this inertia, to get closer to the evidence board. He addressed Malik behind him without bothering to turn around: 'If we want to get permission to do further investigations, there's no room for error. We'll only get one chance.'

Giancarlo ran a nervous hand through his thick hair, sighed and then said: 'Well... if you look at this belt around Paris...'

Giancarlo stopped abruptly and took a step back. His eyes went from the map to the chronological sequence just below it and back to the map. Something had just jumped out at him without him being able to put his finger on it: an imbalance, a dissonance between the two charts. His brain went into overdrive like autofocus moving the lens blocks to get the sharpest possible image. In a fraction of a second, he identified what was wrong.

Something was missing.

Still holding his head in his hands, Malik sensed from Giancarlo's attitude that something new had emerged in front of him. He immediately got up to join him, wondering what he had discovered.

Giancarlo finally broke his silence as he felt Malik approaching: 'Do you think you could number the places where the bodies were found by crime date?'

Malik's eyes lit up. He had just understood what Giancarlo was getting at. Not all the bodies had been discovered immediately after the victim's death—as had been the case with Gabriel—but often several months later. He rushed to the table and grabbed a felt-tip pen. Then, running his finger over the victims one by one, he numbered the places on the map in the chronological order of their death: from the oldest to the most recent.

When he had finished, Malik stood up and took a step back to examine the result, then gave Giancarlo a knowing look.

'He's also methodical in his choice of places when he disposes of his victims…'

Malik put his index finger on the spot where the first 2013 victim was found. He then slid his finger to the second victim and so on until he got to the last 2014 victim.

'2015, nothing, then in 2016, we start from there…'

Malik continued the invisible line, sliding his index finger from one place to the next until he reached the Lac d'Ailette where Gabriel was found.

'Our killer is moving northwards on this belt, counter-clockwise,' he concluded.

'The killer knows the house, our division into

jurisdictions, into districts as well. You were right the other day when you said that he was certainly relying on our lack of coordination: bodies in different districts to avoid any overlap with previous crimes,' added Giancarlo.

'Would it be a *flic*?'

'Maybe…' Giancarlo muttered, rubbing his chin.

Malik continued the exercise, starting from the place where the last 2014 victim was found. He slid his finger slowly up the belt to the north, carefully examining the map of the area. As usual, he articulated his train of thought: 'We are looking for… a body of water, big enough to dispose of a body… easy to get to…He must be able to go back and forth in a few hours… Close to a motorway exit… not too many houses around… so as not to be seen…'

His index finger slipped, returned, hesitated, and finally settled on a stretch of water along the Yonne, level with Montereau, comprising deep basins and stretching over several kilometres.

'There!' announced Malik, full of confidence, 'we have to search from there and downstream for a few kilometres.'

Without hesitation, Giancarlo took out his phone and called the public prosecutor.

16.

16km.

Aghast, Alex looked again at her GPS watch, which confirmed that she had indeed run 16km. She looked around. She had not realised how far she had gone. She did not feel out of breath or tired. She could not even remember what she had been thinking about as she was running. She had seemingly managed to clear her mind. It was dark, and an icy drizzle was coming down from the already threatening black clouds in the sky. Without stopping, she turned back. She would have to run just over ten kilometres to get home.

She thought about the sanction Commissaire Hervé had imposed on her. It was not unfair, far from it. The commissaire had been very lenient towards her. Was it because he understood her conduct? Or with the investigation into little Gabriel's murder gaining momentum, this was not the time to weaken the team? Or because he suspected that she was making others pay for what Masson had done to her while he held her hostage?

It was no secret that she had made a statement like any other victim, giving every detail of the abuse she had

suffered. And the PJ was a place where information circu-
lated quickly. Quicker because the victim in question belonged to the club. Quicker still because the victim was
young, arrogant Alex: an unparalleled and reckless shot,
an investigator who demonstrated flashes of genius. Two
qualities—the envy of all—that had ultimately done her more
harm than good as they had led her into Masson's lair.

She raised her head to the sky to let the drizzle fall on
her face. Had they been revelling with unhealthy curiosity
in the details of her statement, raw and devoid of all emotion? No matter, modesty was not her lot, nor was self-pity.
They could do what they wanted with it. Condescending
compassion or feigned indifference, she had enough to
fight against her demons.

What had shaken her was not having to meet Docteur
Levine twice a week. Quite the contrary. She felt that she
needed her more than ever with this new investigation; it
brought back all this suffering. No, what had shaken her
was her exclusion from the investigation. A child's life was
at stake, hanging on their efficiency, their persistence, their
success. They had little time left, few clues, and she was letting Giancarlo and Malik down at the most delicate moment.

Besides, what was she going to do during this ten-day
suspension on her own? Grind out her dark thoughts and
her guilt? This investigation was her salvation. Save the
child and… and… Was remission at the end of this investigation? She evaded this question. The child had to be
saved.

But what shook her the most was this loss of control, of
consciousness that she had experienced when she threw
herself at the Les Pyramides rapist. She was often

impulsive, even aggressive, but this violence... animal, murderous, which had taken possession of her and blinded her for several minutes, was completely new.

'He is contaminating a past he has never been part of,' Docteur Levine had concluded at their last meeting. Now, it seemed to her the situation was much worse. Masson was contaminating everything: her memories, her dreams, her present. What would be the consequences? Was there a way out of this? Could she even get out of it...?

Alex was still struggling with these thoughts when she saw them. One sat on the bench, his fists deep in his pockets, his head tucked into the collar of his leather jacket to protect himself from the cold. The other, just next to him, perched on the backrest, elbows on his knees, hat pulled down over his head, almost obscuring his eyes. They were waiting for her a few metres from where she lived. Alex slowed down and stopped in front of them. She looked at her GPS watch one last time... 25.6km.

'How do you manage to run in this weather?'

These were the first words Giancarlo had spoken to Alex since she left the Bastion. Their last exchanges had left a bitter taste. She had barely looked at him and slipped away without a word as he held out his hand. Alex had felt terrible for not having bothered to discuss with him what had happened that day. However, she just shrugged her shoulders and replied laconically: 'It makes me feel good.'

'We've got two pieces of news,' Giancarlo announced over Alex's chilly reception, 'one good and one bad. Which do you want to start with?'

'The good one.'

'Malik and I have identified a place in Montereau where the killer could have hidden a body. We have the OK from the public prosecutor to start the search.'

Alex's face lit up and gave Giancarlo one of those all too rare smiles. They looked at each other for a long moment. Was he reading all the words in her mouth that she couldn't get out to apologise for her attitude towards him? Giancarlo's expression vacillated between benevolence and concern.

'And the bad one?' continued Alex.

'The bloke from Les Pyramides... he's been released,' announced Malik.

Alex could not look into his eyes for fear of seeing everything she no longer dared to bear: the mirror of her disintegration. At that very moment, she felt the crack widen a little more. She looked down and sighed, then turned back to Malik with an embarrassed smile: 'I screwed up on this one...'

'Yes,' he confirmed in a word.

And his look was quite different from the one she had feared a few seconds earlier. It was frank and unapologetic.

'I'd like you to do me a favour,' he added.

She looked at him in surprise.

'I'd like you to install an app on your mobile for when you are running like this, alone. It's called *SafeRunning*. You set it with Giancarlo's and my numbers. If you feel in danger, shake your mobile twice, and this app will immediately send us a text message with your GPS location.'

Alex froze in amazement.

'Do you think there will be reprisals?'

Malik nodded and moved on, trying to calm what he felt rising inside her: 'I know you don't need us to defend you but... I know these guys... When they decide to take revenge, they do it in a gang...'

Alex thought about it and finally took her mobile out of her breast pocket, unlocked it and handed it to Malik, who immediately started installing the app.

Alex met Giancarlo's half-surprised, half-amused gaze and shrugged casually.

'*Non ci posso credere*[31]... with him, you don't do anything rash!'

Alex smiled. They stayed a long time together, indifferent to the cold and rain. Malik, concentrating on setting up the app; Giancarlo explaining in detail the latest progress on the investigation; and Alex stretching to relax her muscles after her long run, which had lasted more than two hours. She relished the respite. The round of dark thoughts had subsided.

31 I can't believe it

THE LAST BITE

17.

'I don't have anything really,' answered Alain. He was still investigating David's disappearance. 'There were no witnesses, but it's a busy neighbourhood, full of small shops. The mother didn't want to let go of anything but… how can I put it… I felt uneasy… He's got problems at school… been expelled twice for disciplinary issues with his teachers and classmates… A little troublemaker, in my opinion…'

Alain paused, removed the cigarette that was tucked behind his ear and lit it. He then took a long drag with relish, which he exhaled through his nose with equal pleasure.

'Didn't you quit smoking?' Giancarlo asked bluntly, disgusted both by the smoke and the almost indecent pleasure Alain was taking in his cigarette.

Alain shrugged his shoulders with an air of "I can't help myself".

'I lasted two days… You've got to die of something!'

Giancarlo frowned and decided not to engage in this debate.

'We've got the videos from the surveillance cameras. I'd

say the area is well equipped,' Alain said after exhaling smoke at length. 'You understand, there are quite a few banks in the area.'

'So, you managed to spot it on the videos?'

Alain nodded as he took a final drag, after which he flicked the cigarette butt towards the pavement.

'We see him arriving at the rue Poissonnière level, pass in front of the newspaper kiosk where he stops for a few minutes to look at some magazines. He continues and crosses to rue Fabron. He goes right up the street, turns onto rue Blanche. And there, we lose him… There are no more cameras for a hundred metres. But when we should see him a hundred metres further on, nothing… He's disappeared.'

'Could he have gone somewhere else? Where there are no cameras?'

Alain nodded again.

'Yes, that's what probably happened, and I'm sure that's where and when he disappeared. The kid was on his way to school. So, we should have seen him go by a hundred yards further on… I don't believe in chance; he either ran away or was abducted, and the place where it happened was no accident. It was deliberate.'

'Do you still think he could be a runaway?' asked Giancarlo, which appealed more to his *flic*'s intuition because the evidence did not favour any theory.

'Smart enough to spot surveillance cameras on his route and get out of the way when the coast is clear?'

Alain shrugged and lit a new cigarette: 'These children were born in the age of social networks and consensual voyeurism… You can be filmed with or without your knowledge, at any time, by anyone… in public spaces or private… We have seen videos circulating on the net of minor incidents recorded by surveillance cameras, on a bus, in the street too, which have led to convicting the perpetrators… So no, I wouldn't be surprised if he'd been careful…'

A fine and silent rain greeted Giancarlo and Malik when they came out into the street after interviewing Chloe's mother. Ten-year-old Chloe had disappeared on her way to the conservatoire for her music theory class, which took place every Tuesday at 6:30 p.m. after study hall.

'This is the fourth disappearance we've investigated, and frankly…' Malik shook his head, 'I don't know about you, but as far as I'm concerned, I couldn't tell which disappearance is relevant to our investigation or if we're even on the right track…'

Giancarlo stared at Malik, astonished at this unexpected and surprising standpoint from the man whose attitude had been unfailingly phlegmatic since the beginning of the investigation. Malik had just unleashed his dismay. A crack was appearing in the blind trust he had had up until now in Alex and Giancarlo. The direction they chose always raised more questions than it answered.

Giancarlo understood this feeling; he felt the same way. This investigation was completely unfathomable and slipping through their fingers. He had the unpleasant feeling that they were balancing precariously on a thread spun more from their intuition than from tangible evidence and clues. This truth came back with a vengeance to undermine them with every difficulty they encountered.

How do you explain to Malik that this type of investigation, where you are constantly moving forward in the fog, was rare but all part of the job? You had to know how to deal with them, often by trusting your intuition or simply by a stroke of luck. The outcome was not inevitable, but you could pull them off.

'Or not,' Giancarlo immediately thought to himself. Didn't they say that every *flic* has an unsolved–failed–case in their career that will haunt them for the rest of their life? Like Michel and little Pauline. Alex had often mentioned Pauline's disappearance when they were up to their necks in the Masson case: 'You'll see, this investigation will become our little Pauline.' And then Alex had had one of those famous moments when something "clicks", which he had not wanted to believe in, and which had nevertheless unravelled the investigation at her own expense.

So, if Giancarlo had the same feelings of helplessness and discouragement as Malik that day, his experience enabled him to control them better and, above all, to have confidence in the team they formed. In Alex. He knew that the flash of genius in the Masson case could happen again. If there was one thing that he had learnt from Alex on the Masson case, it was to be open to anything, any event, the slightest sign, and let instinct do the rest.

That's what they were doing, investigating disappearances in search of the child suspended from school and looking for missing bodies from 2015. Giancarlo didn't expect to find a clue or a smoking gun like a note from the god of *flics* saying: "Here you go, it's written on this". You had to search, explore every possible lead and be constantly on the alert. He bitterly regretted that Alex was not there.

How do you pass all this on to Malik? It was time to tell him the whole story about the Masson case.

They took shelter inside a brasserie. Giancarlo spoke a lot, and Malik listened carefully. He understood that everything he had read in the press at the time was far from the truth. The photo that had made such an impression on him hid much more than all the fantasies it aroused in public opinion. It had reinforced in his mind that he had been right to insist on joining this team if he wanted to tackle complex cases: Alex and Giancarlo were the *flics* who would help him become better. He was almost ashamed to have questioned their way of conducting this investigation. It was beyond doubt the one he had always dreamt of, why he had joined the police force and the Crime Squad. Now was the time to prove his worth. Now was the time to believe and be persistent.

THE LAST BITE

18.

It was 8:00 a.m. The day was breaking without enthusiasm over the Montereau basins. By dint of negotiation, Giancarlo had been given what he needed by the public prosecutor. However, this operation made him nervous. He knew that he had used up all his ammunition to get this search and would lose much of the confidence he had painstakingly built up during the whole of his career if the Brigade Aquatique came back empty-handed.

In the euphoria after discovering the Montereau basins a few days earlier, he became convinced beyond doubt that they would find a body there. That morning, as operations got underway, he had reconsidered and now viewed this venture as an extremely risky one. They had rushed headlong into extrapolating the results of a computer programme which, although it had already had several successes in Canada, had not been tested enough in France to be considered infallible.

Giancarlo fumbled mechanically in the inside pocket of his jacket to remind himself that he had not smoked for a year now: no palliative for his anxiety.

Malik stood next to him; his apprehension was

contagious. Jaw clenched, Malik's eyes feverishly darted back and forth from the basins, where divers were starting to get busy, to the car park overlooking them two hundred metres away.

Malik's agitation did not go unnoticed. Giancarlo was about to ask him why he was so tense when he heard a familiar engine. A motorbike came into the car park and slowly moved towards one end, which offered a perfect view of the operation in progress. Alex's bike: a black Ducati Monster.

Giancarlo turned sharply to Malik, who seemed to have relaxed suddenly. He then realised that Malik had told Alex the search would take place today. She had been suspended and was not supposed to be here. Giancarlo ran his hand nervously over his growing stubble. He should have been angry, but he was reassured deep down that she was there. For form's sake, he cast a disapproving look at Malik, who made amends by shrugging apologetically before turning his head away to focus all his attention on the divers in front of them.

Giancarlo's eyes returned to the motorbike, which finally stopped. Alex did not remove her helmet or raise the visor. She straightened up, switched off the engine and waited. She looked like a black angel, motionless and upright on her Ducati.

The operations took time and played on Giancarlo's nerves as he watched each of the divers' ascents, growing impatient as he saw nothing coming up with them. The more time passed and the closer it got to the end of the morning, the more discouraged he became.

Then he heard the Ducati engine roar. He turned and saw Alex slowly backing up and heading for the exit. She sped away. Did she think there was no hope and leave the scene? Giancarlo saw that the boats sounding the basin bottom were heading further downstream. He watched the motorbike accelerate dramatically along the road that ran alongside the basins, slow down and stop in a car park further on, overlooking the divers. Alex had decided to follow them.

Operations were moving steadily, inexorably approaching the search area's perimeter without finding a single body. This investigation still caught them off guard, and they were missing their only shot.

Just as Giancarlo was about to call it a day, a diver surfaced and waved to the zodiac following him a few metres upstream. The boat accelerated to join him. The diver and the police officers on board stayed talking for a while. Then the diver resubmerged and, after what seemed like an eternity, he came up with a package in his arms: a black bin bag containing what looked like a body.

Giancarlo squinted to get a better look at the shape of the package as they hoisted it aboard. He exchanged an incredulous look with Malik. They spontaneously turned to Alex, who slowly turned her head towards them at the same time. And although they couldn't see the expression on her face hidden under her motorbike helmet, they knew she shared their perplexity.

The body, perfectly moulded in the black bin bag, still had all its limbs.

THE LAST BITE

19.

'You belong to me, now and forever. This mark is my seal,' he announced coldly, bright red blood dripping from his mouth.

Alex jumped out of bed screaming for her life, threw herself on all fours and cowered in the corner of her room. She scratched desperately at the wall to escape the room, but she couldn't get out no matter how hard she scratched. Frantically she scratched and scratched again.

'Help me... please help me...' she sobbed.

She turned around and pressed her back against the wall. Breathing hard, her eyes petrified, she looked for another way out when slowly, emerging from her nightmare, she finally recognised the walls of her room. 'Oh God, please make it stop!' she thought as she heard a distant thud. Still disoriented, she clung to the sound to bring herself irrevocably back to reality and regain her composure. She blinked and looked around. Yes, everything was there, the familiar objects, the bed, her bed, gutted, the sheets thrown on either side, her bathrobe lying on the floor. She was at home, in her room. She listened carefully and realised that someone was banging on the door.

'Hey! Are you alright?!'

She looked around once more, her eyes everywhere. Yes, she was in her room. And she was alone.

There was still shouting and banging at the door. Alex struggled to her feet, her legs like jelly. She picked up her bathrobe, quickly put it on, and staggered to the front door, shouting: 'It's fine! It's fine!'

When she opened the door, she found her young neighbour looking at her dumbfounded and concerned.

'You scared the shit out of me! You were screaming like someone was killing you!' he explained, visibly upset.

'It was a nightmare... I'm sorry... It was just a nightmare... It's fine now... I'm sorry,' she stammered, trying to smile at him reassuringly.

After closing the door, Alex slowly made her way to the bathroom, discarded her bathrobe, stepped into the shower, and cried her heart out.

'This investigation is upsetting you. I understand that this is not easy to hear, but I need to be frank and direct with you... Your condition may have altered your judgement, even completely distorted it. You're working on instinct. More than that, you're working on empathy. You need to stand back from this investigation. It will seem extremely difficult, but I'm afraid you don't have the capacity right now, Mademoiselle Ramblay.'

Docteur Levine looked at Alex with great firmness and continued: 'I may be bound by medical confidentiality, but I can write an opinion, and I will not hesitate to intervene if you don't. So, I urge you: divest yourself of this investigation.'

Alex received this last sentence like a punch in the gut.

They stared at each other for a long time until Docteur Levine spoke more softly: 'You must understand that I am not a surgeon who will cut out your brain, extract the trauma that is slowly destroying you, and sew it back together with a nice scar. I'm here to help you understand how to unravel your problems, but you're the only one who can act. You must stop waiting and telling yourself that these traumatic memories will fade away with time and that everything will work out.'

Alex remained silent, overwhelmed by Docteur Levine's words, still stunned by the previous day's nightmare, which had never been so intense. All she could do was nod like a docile child.

Docteur Levine continued: 'Mademoiselle Ramblay... I'm aware that what I'm asking of you is very difficult, but it's an essential step that will enable us to find the keys to your reconstruction.'

Even before she heard the rest, Alex had already understood what Docteur Levine was going to ask of her, something she had flatly refused to do. She had agreed to share her statements, paid lip service to some of the questions but never been able to go beyond a factual and neutral description of what she had suffered seven years earlier.

'I'm going to need you to tell me exactly what happened during the four days you were locked up. I want your side of the story,' Docteur Levine said, emphasising the word "your", 'Alex's side... not Capitaine Ramblay's.'

Docteur Levine added: 'I know that this is insurmountable for you, terribly painful, but to be able to reprocess and decondition the trauma that you have experienced, we need to re-access it. There's a protocol that has been tested successfully on victims of terrorist attacks. Coupled with specific drug treatment, we will be able to bring back these memories in a state of altered consciousness and significantly reduce how you feel them. I can assure you of this. I ask you to trust me.'

Alex's face was tense, her jaw tight. She nodded, knowing full well that she wouldn't have the strength. To have felt Masson so real and so present with her last night still chilled her blood, body, and soul.

Still, she needed to recover.

At least try.

She could never give up the investigation.

20.

It was precisely 8:33 a.m. Heavy, sticky rain was falling in Paris. Giancarlo and Malik were in the autopsy room at the IML.

Wiser for the first experience, Malik quickly grabbed his notebook to concentrate on taking notes and distract himself from what was about to unfold before his eyes in the minutes that followed. He heard the familiar creak of trolley wheels. The stench of rotting flesh that went with the body was suffocating him before it had even been uncovered. It became abundantly clear he was unaccustomed to this. He was about to turn away when Giancarlo passed him his small pot of camphor balm, which he feverishly plastered around his nose. He cautiously reclosed it and handed it back to Giancarlo, who was absorbed in examining the body that had just arrived and ignored him.

On the verge of fainting, Malik could only vaguely hear Giancarlo and Docteur Saranches' voices. He tried to fight the feeling of nausea that rose from his stomach to his throat. He patted Giancarlo's arm again. This time Giancarlo barely turned his head, took the small jar of ointment back from him, and absentmindedly stuffed it into his jacket pocket.

Malik carefully avoided looking at the body. His eyes went from his notebook to Docteur Saranches' face and then to the intern taking pictures of the victim from every angle.

Docteur Saranches dress and demeanour were as neat and lively as the last time they had met her. She looked more like a TV cook show host with her voluminous bun, red tortoiseshell glasses, small fleshy mouth, and decidedly academic tone. It was much easier for Malik to concentrate on the graceful movement of her lips than the rotting body.

'Is this victim related to the one at Lac d'Ailette, Capitaine Ranieri?'

'That is what we think.'

'Well, let's start. We are dealing with a white female child. The body is reasonably well preserved. I'll need the exact location they found the body to estimate the date of death as accurately as possible.'

'We found her at the bottom of a basin fed by the Yonne at Montereau, about 100 kilometres southeast of Paris. The body was weighted down and held at a depth of more than four metres,' said Giancarlo.

Docteur Saranches nodded and stood pensively for a moment before continuing her methodical examination of the child between her intern's compulsive flashes.

When Malik felt better, he, at last, tried to look at the body. He had been reluctant to visualise the slightest fragment despite all the detailed information he had noted since the autopsy began.

Malik proceeded to look step by step, glances at first, then for longer and longer, giving his brain time to get used to the monstrosity–much as you blink to get used to light that is too bright. Finally, he managed to look at it in its entirety.

It was a deformed body: the face swollen, the eyelids looked about to burst, and the skin had a greenish hue. The skull still had long, fair strands of hair attached, and despite all the blistered skin, Malik could spot the incision in the carotid artery at the base of the neck from which she had bled out.

Docteur Saranches had also pointed out earlier that she had found the same mark on the back of the skull: a blow from a blunt object. The child had been knocked unconscious before her throat was methodically slit, the same as Gabriel.

There were no bite marks, which did not unsettle them, as the bites were recent in the killer's modus operandi: for the last three victims.

Malik let his gaze slide over the child's arms and legs, to which a few shreds of flesh clung, blackened by putrefaction, as if the killer had chosen to devour the corpse starting with the tenderest parts. When his eyes fell on the child's trunk, he was overwhelmed by fear, which compressed his chest and took his breath away.

The child had been disembowelled, gutted: liver, stomach, intestines, and heart. From the bladder to the lungs, there was nothing left.

Malik felt the ground sway under his feet. He was regretting his boldness when a blinding flash of light hit him like an electric shock. He blinked and discovered Docteur Saranches' intern looking at him, her eyes distorted by the thick lenses of her glasses. Lowering her camera, she said to him in a mocking tone: 'I'll attach it as an appendix to the report. You can keep it to look at in a few years!'

The intern chuckled but quickly pulled herself together under Docteur Saranches' reproachful gaze.

'The job done here is quite remarkable,' she continued. 'The abdominal wall has been incised very cleanly–crosswise–here and there to allow the organs as already noted to be removed. The removal is also surprisingly precise. Your killer is very meticulous and has a highly detailed knowledge of the human body.'

'Do you think he could be a doctor?' asked Giancarlo.

'Yes, he could be. In any case, he has all the qualities, Capitaine Ranieri.'

Docteur Saranches paused for a few seconds, looking thoughtful.

'It's not very scientific what I'm going to say here... but...'

Giancarlo and Malik looked up from their respective notebooks, the intern stopped machine-gunning the body, and all three stood motionless, hanging on Docteur Saranches' every word.

'In the way he mutilates, he shows great care and respect for his victims.'

21.

Alex pounded the streets for almost two hours. Her eyes veiled in the colours of the mist that had settled over Paris after the storm. Her ears were saturated with music to drown out her thoughts. She clung to the pavement as she strode along, unable to see very far in front of her.

When Alex was a few metres from home, she decelerated gradually, took off her headphones, annoyed. She stopped her GPS watch and began walking to lower her heart rate. The run had been for nothing as Alex could still feel that her body was tense. She forced herself to relax her arms and shoulders. The sessions with Docteur Levine had turned into mental torture. Alex could feel her whole body working with her unconscious to build walls around the memories she wanted to keep buried. Lava flowed into her with each breach Docteur Levine opened, burning everything in its path. Wasn't the purpose of these sessions to release her, to relieve her?

Malik was waiting, perched on the back of the bench in front of where she lived as usual. His head turned so that she could not make out his face. He had that casual, determined attitude that was now familiar to her. Malik was a bright, straightforward young man. Even though he was very mature, he still wore a certain innocence on his face, the innocence of someone whose integrity was never compromised.

Malik turned around and caught Alex looking straight at him. He nodded in greeting and, without taking his eyes off her, let her come to him.

'Isn't Giancarlo here?'

'He should be back soon. He had to make one last phone call.'

Without beating around the bush, Malik moved straight to the autopsy report. Alex listened, lost in thought. Was the killer a medical professional? Was he a doctor, a psychopathic surgeon, or even a failed surgeon? He respected his victims. Yes, that is what she had felt, but the bites said it went beyond respect: he loved his victims. They belonged to him.

What puzzled her was this unexpected mutilation, which was at odds with those of the other victims. Their limbs were severed, but this girl had been disembowelled. Her arms and legs were left untouched. Why?

She did not realise that Malik had suddenly fallen silent. He had stopped mid-sentence. His breathing had suddenly become more muffled like an animal sensing imminent danger.

The stroke was soft and gentle as Malik touched her hand. He was looking up the street. He mechanically reached for his holster, only to curse himself for having put it in his locker along with his gun before leaving the Bastion earlier. His jaw tightened. He nodded to Alex to look to her left, which she did.

There were about ten of them. Between fourteen and

twenty years old. They were about a hundred metres away and moving slowly towards them. Alex immediately recognised the Les Pyramides rapist, a menacing look on his face. Malik had been right: he was coming for revenge, and he was coming in a gang. It was his moment, and the "whore" was going to regret attacking him.

'Alex, beat it. Go and call for help,' Malik urged her through clenched teeth.

Alex could not take her eyes off the horde advancing towards them. And even though they were careful to hide it behind their backs or under their clothes, she could see that they were all armed–knuckledusters, iron bars, switchblades. Her jaw tightened. Her body stiffened.

'You don't know me very well, Malik. No way, I couldn't live with myself. And that's all I have left.'

Alex's tone of voice was curt, leaving no room for discussion. They exchanged a long look, sizing each other up, calculating their respective tenacity.

'Good,' conceded Malik. 'Now's the time to shake your phone, and we'll just have to hope that Giancarlo isn't too far away.'

Alex didn't wait for him to finish the sentence. She gave her mobile two shakes, and they instantly heard Malik's phone beeping. If he had just got a text from the *SafeRunning* app, Giancarlo would have it too, along with Alex's GPS coordinates.

They would have to hold out until he arrived.

Malik slowly got down from the bench and pulled the zip of his jacket up to his neck, a closed expression on his face. Alex swallowed. She was in a t-shirt and leggings; she had no protection against blows.

These youths advancing towards them were full of

anger and aggression. They drew their weapons in unison a few metres away and rushed at them without warning.

Malik stood in front of Alex and used his body to block the first volley of blows. They soon found themselves surrounded, blows coming at them from all sides. They countered the ferocity of these youths with their mastery and fighting techniques. Malik threw himself on the gang leader. Galvanised by his rage for revenge, he was by far the most dangerous. Alex distributed kicks and elbowing aimed at Adam's apples or kneecaps. But, rapidly overwhelmed by the number of aggressors, a baseball bat suddenly belted her in the ribs, and she was thrown violently against the bench.

Stunned by the shock, she just had the reflex to raise her arm to protect her face from the knife stabs that were coming at her. The blade slid down her forearm, cutting deep into her flesh and to the bone. The pain sent an electric shock through her arm, and she screamed. The spurt of blood sent the attacker reeling backwards, giving her time to get to her feet and sweep him off his with a kick to the chin that sent him crashing to the ground.

Before she had time to rejoice, a punch to the jaw knocked her to the ground senseless. Still lying on the pavement, she was kicked in the stomach, which took her breath away and caused her to gasp in pain. Her entire body was in nothing but agony.

'Leave her to me. I fucking want to finish this whore!'

The beating stopped. Blood was streaming down her face. She opened her eyes, and, despite her vision blurred by her blood, she managed to spot Malik lying on the pavement. His body looked as limp as a rag doll, shaken with spasms.

And they continued to go at him fiercely and unrelentingly.

Then she spotted a puddle of thick, dark red liquid beneath Malik's head growing slowly on the pavement.

'Leave him be…' she pleaded for the first time in seven years.

Her voice faded into nothing. Despite all her will and desire to save Malik, Alex remained on the ground, drained of strength and unable to get up.

A score of menacing trainers closed in around her, coming to rest a few inches from her face.

'Now it's your turn, you dirty bitch!' one of the youths spat at her.

In one last effort, Alex tried to flex her whole body, the better to withstand the blows about to rain down on her when she heard a click.

A click she knew well.

The click of a SIG Sauer Pro 2340 being cocked.

A stony silence fell until an authoritative voice with a harsh tone announced coldly: 'You touch one hair on her head, and I'll blow your face off, *figlio di putana*[32].'

With that, Alex fainted.

---

32 You son of a bitch

THE LAST BITE

22.

Giancarlo drove Alex home in their unmarked car. She had signed a self-discharge form to leave the hospital that evening against doctors' advice. Her jaw was swollen where she had been punched and knocked to the ground. The cut on her eyebrow had been closed with simple steri-strips. The gash on her forearm, on the other hand, had required more than forty stitches from wrist to elbow. Her chest X-rays had revealed two cracked ribs for which there was nothing to be done but wait for them to knit themselves back together again. Her stomach hurt too, but the doctors had reassured her—she was doing well—the organs were not affected. She would have to be patient: nausea and bruising for a few days.

The mood in the car on the way home was sombre. Alex and Giancarlo had left the hospital with a mental image of Malik in intensive care, inanimate, assisted by a whole lot of noisy and unnerving medical equipment keeping him alive.

A few hours earlier, she had padded softly into the intensive care unit. She had approached Malik and stroked his hand for quite a while. Malik, who had used his body without fear or reproach to prevent the worst at his own expense. The doctors had put him in an artificial coma to spare him too much suffering.

Alex closed her eyes and let herself lean against the car door window. She was losing her footing and could feel herself sinking.

When Giancarlo turned off the engine, she was still drowsy. He let her sleep, and when she finally woke up, he walked her to her apartment. They paused on each floor because of the nausea that overwhelmed her and made her unsteady. Once inside it, Giancarlo left her alone in the small living room and went to the kitchen.

Alex staggered to the window and leant against the recess, wincing in pain.

'I've made some coffee,' Giancarlo announced, putting the still steaming cup on the coffee table to be within easy reach.

'How do you feel?' he asked as he gently tucked a strand of hair behind her ear to clear her face.

'For seven years now, my life has been shit, and today on top of that, I'm ashamed. I'm ashamed because it's all my fault…'

Alex turned her face sharply towards Giancarlo and looked straight into his eyes. No tears, just anger in hers. She stared straight into his, her gaze fevered, daring him to say otherwise, provoking him into frankness.

'I don't think it was you that beat up Malik, Alex.'

'Don't treat me like a fool, Giancarlo! Of course not! But look at me, dammit! Look what I've become! I'm all skin and bones.'

Despite the pain, she grabbed her t-shirt by the collar, drawing it into her clenched fists as if stretching her emaciated body's skin to prove that there was indeed nothing left between the skin and bones.

'I live alone, I am alone… and who would want me when I can't even look at myself in the mirror. Giancarlo, he branded me. And even if he's rotting in prison now, he won. Yes, I still belong to him as I can't give myself to anyone else! Look, look what he did to me!" she cried, her throat choked with sobs and snot dripping from her nose.

'There!' she shouted, pulling up the sleeve of her shirt to her armpit.

'There!' she shouted again, pulling her shirt up over her stomach and then to her neck.

'There!' she said, her voice trembling as she pulled down her bra to reveal the extensively scarified curve of her breast.

Giancarlo stared at her, dumbfounded by the swollen and unsightly scars, like the one around her mouth he had learnt not to see anymore. He saw these bites when he broke down the door of the room in which she had been held for four days, seven years earlier. He would never forget that vision: Alex handcuffed to a filthy bed, covered in her own crusty, dried blood, moaning in pain, like one huge gaping wound.

These images suddenly flashed through his mind, just as vivid and unbearable as Alex's suffering today. She had just given him a resounding slap in the face, and he realised that while he could wipe those images from his mind with the blink of an eye, Alex could not. She had been carrying them around with her for seven years, embedded in her skin. And this unbearable truth he had carefully pushed aside until today exploded in his face.

'*Smettila*[33]! Stop!' he shouted in turn, grabbing Alex's hands now pulling on her leggings to continue the unbearable inventory. But Alex was as if possessed by demons of a past that were even more painful because it was so relentlessly alive.

Giancarlo shook her by the shoulders to bring her to her senses. They were staring at each other, the tension between them becoming stifling. They were standing on a boundary edge neither had ever wanted to cross, which had become fragile over the last few years and had just cracked before their astonished eyes. Giancarlo looked deep into Alex's eyes and realised the depth of her despair behind her fury. Overwhelmed, he pulled her roughly into a hug. He held her tightly despite the broken ribs, despite the pain because he had to show her that he was there. For her. If he could , to smother the pain just waiting to spew forth from her entire being but unable to find a way out.

Alex stifled a gasp and surrendered herself entirely to this embrace. Her muscles finally relaxed, and all self-restraint collapsed: she began to scream, sob, scream again. The pain, the anger, the rage and all her powerlessness to survive this past.

They remained in each other's arms until Alex had calmed down completely. She gently released herself from Giancarlo's embrace and, wiping her tear-stained, snotty face with the back of her sleeves, looked into his eyes. After such an intimate sharing, this frank and unabashed gaze unsettled Giancarlo. Alex smiled awkwardly and finally broke the silence: 'Fortunately, I still go out a bit in the evening. I see Michel. A retired *flic* who's lost the plot…'

33 *Stop that!*

23.

'Giancarlo, we need to ask ourselves the right questions,' Alex declared.

Her suspension had been cut short at Giancarlo's express request because Malik was still in the hospital. So, she had been able to join Giancarlo the next day at the Bastion to lend him a hand and continue the investigation. Having her close to him in this office reassured him, even if he knew she was unwell. Alex could go off the rails at any moment; he would have to watch her like milk on the stove. Even so, he told himself, she was better off being busy doing what she knew best than home alone with her dark thoughts.

Alex stood in front of the evidence board and read the additions to it during her absence. In the space of a few days, it had filled up completely and was about to overflow. Who could have predicted the magnitude of this investigation? Gabriel was now one of a string of victims. All had been murdered and mutilated except for one whose life was on hold. And that one was among the photos Alex was examining. Her gaze shifted to the chronological sequence: they had only two days left.

Two days until the date Salvac had calculated for the next crime. They did not have complete confidence in Salvac, but the discovery of the Montereau body and Docteur Saranches' confirmation that the presumed death went back to 2015 had tipped the balance in favour of artificial intelligence. Even if the mutilations were not the same, the bin bags, the blows to the back of the skull and severed carotid arteries were still sufficiently discriminating elements. The discovery of the body in Montereau confirmed the modus operandi, and they had a date to go on for the next one.

Nevertheless, if Salvac had put them on the right track, it was only telling them what the data at its disposal and the mathematical algorithms could say. The rest they had to find out for themselves. And looking at all the photos, graphs and clues, Alex realised that they were still missing something vital.

'How does he choose his victims?' Alex asked aloud, her words reverberating around the room like an echo of their uncertainties.

They went through all the files again, looking at the disappearance locations, the dates. Did they correspond to a particular day, a solstice, a full moon? A victim profile might have surfaced based on age, social condition, belonging to a single-parent family, but as for the rest, no other link emerged: the children did not know each other, did not live in the same neighbourhood, nor did they attend the same school.

Giancarlo and Malik had investigated all the potential victims but had been unable to reach a decision. Only one case had not been ruled out, Julie's. Giancarlo was still waiting for the results of the research he had requested.

The worktable now looked like a battlefield. Giancarlo was swaying precariously in his chair. Alex was leaning her elbows on the table, holding her head in her hands, trying to drown out the countdown clock's ticking tormenting her inside. The telephone ring shook away their thoughts with a certain amount of relief.

Giancarlo unfolded his numb body and picked up the receiver. Alex followed him with her eyes, hung on his every word, desperately hoping for something new.

Giancarlo hung up the phone.

His face lighting up, he announced: 'It was forensics. They analysed the CCTV footage, and they have found images of Julie on the day she disappeared!'

Alex stood up abruptly, triggering a sharp twinge in her ribs and twisting her face in pain. They both grabbed their jackets, and Giancarlo added as they left the office: 'On the video, you can see someone approaching her, just before she went astray.'

'If I move forward a little...that's it... there! You see, she's walking up the street, she's got her back turned and then she's going to turn her head to look at the shop window. That's when you can recognise her. That's it... there!'

'Pause, please,' cut in Giancarlo.

Alex and Giancarlo leaned over to get a better look at the profile of the child who had just turned her head.

'The clothes match those reported by the mother,' the technician pointed out.

'Has the mother identified her daughter on the video?'

'Not yet. The investigating officer wanted you to see it first.'

Alex took a long look at the child's profile. There was no

doubt that it was Julie, a plump young girl with a physique languishing in childhood and a small snub nose. Alex signalled to the technician to continue the playback.

Julie is walking slowly down the sloping street. Julie walks looking down at her feet like all children. A woman suddenly enters the camera's field of view a few metres behind the girl and hurries towards her.

Alex instantly thought of Gabriel and the only witness statement collected by investigators at the time. It had not been deemed sufficiently reliable but had nevertheless reported that Gabriel had been approached by a "clean" woman in her fifties.

In the video, the woman can be seen from behind. It was hard to tell her age, but she matched the description in the statement from Gabriel's disappearance: she was well dressed and quite feminine in a dark skirt and loafers, wearing a well-cut beige woollen jacket, her mid-length hair neatly trimmed.

When the stranger reaches Julie, the child turns towards her and smiles shyly. The stranger must be addressing her because Julie remains silent with an attentive expression on her face. Then her facial expression becomes anxious, and she responds to the woman; she seems to be asking her a question. Her face relaxes as the stranger presses her arm comfortingly. Finally, the stranger wraps her arm around Julie's shoulders, holding her close. They walk up the street and turn at the intersection.

The video stopped abruptly, leaving Alex and Giancarlo speechless. At no time could they see the face of the unknown woman taking Julie with her.

'I know it's frustrating, but the street they're walking down is not equipped with a surveillance camera. We scream about privacy when we hear about cameras in public spaces–I'm the first. But we wish they were everywhere when faced with cases like this!'

Alex sidestepped the debate to return to their investigation and what they had just seen. They had not yet got everything out of the recording: 'Were you able to make out what Julie was saying to this stranger?'

'She doesn't say much…'

'Yes, but it's important,' Alex cut in sharply.

The technician nodded, taken aback. Suddenly, struck by an epiphany, he got up and disappeared into one of the neighbouring offices. He returned a few minutes later, accompanied by a woman in her forties with a pleasant smile.

'Meet Nathalie, Nathalie can lip-read.'

'My son is hard of hearing,' she felt compelled to say.

Nathalie took the technician's place in front of the screen. They played back to her the extract where Julie was talking to the unknown woman.

'It's not obvious… she's mumbling…' announced Nathalie, clicking her tongue. 'Could you play it again for me, please?'

'Again,' Nathalie repeated, bringing her face close to the screen until the tip of her nose touched it.

The extract lasted only two or three seconds. Nathalie looked at it a good ten times before giving up and sitting back in her seat.

'I'm not one hundred per cent sure… but I think the little one asks her: "Mum? Is it serious?"'

Alex couldn't relax. The ball of nerves sitting in the pit of her stomach throbbed dangerously. She had even handed over the wheel to Giancarlo when they returned to the

Bastion.

'The monsters!' she finally burst out, thumping the dashboard several times, which triggered a searing wave of pain in her sides that took her breath away. 'Can you believe it?!' she continued, 'Using their mothers to quietly kidnap them... Real scum!'

'Alex... easy, girl. Now is not the time to crack up, OK? I need you. We're going to go back to the Bastion. So, no funny business, OK? I don't need to remind you that only yesterday, you were on suspension again. I need you on this investigation, OK?'

Alex took a long breath as she closed her eyes.

Giancarlo's gaze went nervously from the road to Alex.

'Like milk on the stove,' he reminded himself.

'Alex, we're agreed there are at least two of them, *chiaro*[34]?'

Alex understood that Giancarlo was talking about the perpetrators.

'Yes, I don't see a woman mutilating children like that. Poisoning them maybe, but killing and dismembering them like that... It doesn't feel right...' she agreed. 'In any case, I'm convinced of one thing after seeing the video...'

Giancarlo was looking at Alex questioningly when she let out: 'Julie knew this woman. It's clear from the images that she recognises her.'

34 Clear?

24.

Alex was in the Bastion self-service, stood perplexed in front of the day's specials. She was busily scrutinising the chilled contents of two large zinc trays when Danny came out of the kitchen to greet her. She recognised overcooked calf liver slices with parsley in the first and kidneys swimming in a brown, greasy sauce in the second. Danny was chattering away, as usual, trying to get Alex's attention. Despite his best efforts, he could see that she was mesmerised by the dishes of the day.

'Well, then, my dear, have you never seen calf's liver before or don't you know which way to go?'

Danny's voice finally reached Alex and pulled her from her thoughts.

'Danny, is this all we have to eat today? I know I'm a bit late but, could I have a grilled steak?'

He put his hands on his hips and laughed out loud: 'You're making a face, my dear! Sorry, no more steak in the kitchen... but you know, beef is like pork, everything's good! And when it's lean, you can always eat the offal... It's tasty and good for your health. You'd be surprised!'

Danny continued talking in his cheerful tone, but Alex

was no longer listening. Did he realise that even though she was staring at him with her eyes wide open, they were no longer seeing him? Words swelled and danced in Alex's head, dancing in a strange round: "everything in beef is good". Her pupils shrank, and Danny disappeared altogether: "when it's lean, you can always eat the offal". The round of words accelerated, intensified, and tumbled into a great stampede against the walls of her skull: "everything is good", "when it's lean", "offal".

'You look pale... are you alright?' inquired Danny.

Alex gasped and refocused on Danny staring at her.

'Yes, I need to talk to Giancarlo. *Ciao*[35] Danny,' she replied distractedly.

Alex turned on her heels and ran out of the dining hall, despite the pain throbbing in her ribs. She had just realised what the killer did to the children, what he did with their mutilated limbs, and why he kept them with him for so long before getting rid of them.

Giancarlo was in the middle of reviewing the victims' files when Alex swept into the office. He looked up to see her catching her breath, her eyes glowing. He knew at once that she had something vital to tell him. But before she could even open her mouth, the phone rang. They both froze: what was going on? This desperately lacklustre investigation had been wavering all day, like an old seismograph stylus at the first signs of an earthquake. The ringing continued to resonate in the office, insistent. How often had they sat in that office at the end of the corridor? On their own, disillusioned by the lack of clues, waiting for a

35 'bye

phone call? From forensics, from the IML, or from anyone else connected with this investigation.

When Giancarlo picked up the phone, he fixed his eyes firmly on Alex's as though to ensure that she wouldn't vanish into thin air with her valuable information.

'Capitaine Ranieri? It's Docteur Saranches speaking. I am just finalising the autopsy report on the Montereau basin victim and… You remember I told you that the mutilations were clean and carried out methodically,' Docteur Saranches sounded embarrassed and paused for a long moment. 'Well, the more I look at the photos, particularly those of the Lac d'Ailette victim, the more I think there's an alternative…'

Giancarlo was trying to control his nerves and impatience, hanging onto the phone and Docteur Saranches' every word. What a palaver. Can't we get to the point?

'Yes, well?' he encouraged her.

'I'd say he's a butcher,' she asserted. 'He doesn't amputate his victims; he cuts up pieces of meat.'

When Giancarlo hung up, he was confused, not sure what to make of this information. Alex still stood at the end of his gaze, motionless though inwardly seething.

'Tell me and make it brief, *per piacere*[36],' he asked her, putting his phone on the table.

'He eats them, Giancarlo! He fattens them up, chops them up, and eats them! As he would a leg of lamb or sweetbreads!'

Giancarlo's eyes opened wide: a cannibal? The very idea appalled him.

Cases of killers with proven acts of anthropophagy were

---

36 Please

exceedingly rare in France. The last case went back as far as 2007: an inmate in Rouen prison savagely killed one of his fellow inmates, then ate a piece of his lung, part raw and the rest cooked with a pinch of garlic, rice, and shallots. Then there was the Japanese student who had devoured part of his girlfriend in Paris in 1981. More than a century and a half after the conviction and execution in 1824 of Antoine Léger, the first notorious French cannibal. But Giancarlo knew that you needed more than statistics to get to grips with a crime. Not so surprising, society is increasingly manufacturing and vomiting out criminals with deviant psychopathology.

Stunned and at the same time encouraged by this twist in their investigation, he turned to the evidence board. He looked for a moment at the pinned-up photos of the victims. Something he had never noticed before now seemed obvious: they all had the chubby, round faces of over-indulged pre-pubescent children who spent their solitary moments digging through the kitchen cupboards and drinking sodas. He thought again about the bite marks, which were an expression of sexual drive, of criminals' desire to possess their victims, just like anthropophagy.

Well, Docteur Saranches' and Alex's two hypotheses fitted together perfectly.

Could it be possible?

Giancarlo ran his hand nervously through his hair. Then slowly, just long enough to unfold his frame, he stood up and walked over to the board. Using a red marker pen, he added left-handed: Butcher? Cannibal?

Alex was contemplating all the elements pinned on the board just behind him. Her gaze first lingered on the Salvac graphics annotated here and there in coloured felt-tip pen.

Then her illegible scrawl, Malik's freehand lines, arrows and circles, the words she had added in capitals after watching the security camera videos: "KNEW THE KIDNAPPER", "WOMAN 50 AUBURN", "2 PEOPLE? COUPLE?". And finally, Giancarlo's clumsy handwriting, a reflection of his uncertainty and doubts.

Her vision blurred.

Something more imperceptible had just appeared.

Still underexposed, blurred in outline, two shadows stood out: those of the killer and his accomplice.

Strangely, Alex felt neither disgust nor horror at their being child eaters, which momentarily worried her as she turned the pages of the autopsy reports, looking for information that would confirm her hunch.

She had been in a state of psychological chaos since the investigation began. It made her lose control of her emotions and, above all, her composure, essential in this type of investigation.

The intuition that had just struck her at the self-service seemed to put her mind at ease somewhat, anchoring it afresh not on Julie, held captive, in distress and at the mercy of her torturers, but on resolving the enigma that surrounded this investigation. The images of a bloodless, moaning child begging for help that Alex was powerless to give and that tormented her so violently were replaced in her mind by a jigsaw puzzle. Some of the pieces had just lit up, suddenly fitting together perfectly, calling for others to follow.

She quickly found what she was looking for, marked the data with a red cross in the margin and moved on to the second file, then the third, and so on, removing some of the pages, annotating the relevant information each time. A feeling of fulfilment, almost warmth, filled her. And it had been a long time since this had happened. No, she hadn't gone completely off the rails. Not yet. She was still a good *flic*. They were on the right track; she was sure of that now. Everything matched perfectly: Docteur Saranches' findings, the autopsy reports.

She approached Giancarlo, who was sat in front of the window, thinking. It was raining gently outside without affecting the bustle in the street. People seemed in no more or less of a hurry, whether they were dry under an umbrella or soaked to the skin, and the cars were still moving briskly.

Alex handed him the sheets. He barely glanced at them.

'Triglyceride levels are high, which indicates that their livers were particularly stressed before death. The children are all initially healthy. If we compare the weights of some of them, before the abduction and... estimated by the post-mortem examiners, we can see that they have all put on between two and four kilos.'

Alex waved the sheets under Giancarlo's nose, who continued to ignore them.

'And the little girl from Montereau? She was just skin and bones, and it wasn't due to the time spent in the water, at that depth and temperature. The medical examiner said the body was well preserved,' he objected.

'In the case of the Montereau body, I think the little girl refused to eat; she didn't play their game. They make them believe that something has happened to their mum, that she's ill and, evidently, that they'll take care of them until she recovers... The little girl in Montereau will have been too affected by her mum's absence and alleged illness and will have refused to eat... All that remained was the... offal.'

Giancarlo shook his head. Alex's hypothesis was corroborated by Docteur Saranches. The whole thing was beyond him. Alex seemed to be more interested in finding evidence to support her theory than in using evidence to deduce a motive. He heard Alex's arguments but still had his doubts. This cannibalism business didn't thrill him, and something deep inside him didn't buy it. He watched Alex dive back into the reports. Her look was feverish, her expression resolute. Was she right? Yet again… He couldn't help but think back to the Masson case. She had guessed much earlier than he had. At that time, he had had the same misgivings, which was why she had decided to forge ahead on her own and throw herself into the monster's jaws. It had taken Giancarlo four days to find her.

Alex looked up. Their eyes met. For a moment, Alex understood what was going on in Giancarlo's head. No, he was unconvinced. Was he going to desert her again?

Seconds ran into minutes. They both held each other's gaze. Giancarlo thought back again to Alex's emaciated frame. To all the bites covering her body when he had discovered her on that soiled bed in Masson's room. Some of them were still raw and had become the scars that dotted her body with pale blisters, purple for the deeper ones. She had revealed these scars to him after discharging herself from the hospital and he could no longer ignore them. Just after the Masson affair, when she'd gone back to work, he'd systematically avoided looking at the one around her mouth, for her sake and his own, because it brought him back to his guilt over having deserted her. He could see that most people who saw her again or met her for the first time would stare shamelessly at the left corner of her mouth. He noted she surreptitiously turned her face away but would never lower her eyes. Could he be missing a crucial lead again, as indeed he had seven years earlier?

Giancarlo took a deep breath and made his decision: 'Now we have to find their hideout.'

Alex nodded and smiled, and in the depths of her eyes, Giancarlo saw great relief. But he remained clear-headed: it was for her and her alone that he had committed himself.

25.

Alex and Giancarlo were walking along the cobbled streets of the Mouzaïa district in the 19th arrondissement. If you had not known they were from the Crime Squad, you might have thought they were a couple of tourists discovering a new neighbourhood. It was unclear whether they were trying to find their way or, unconsciously, delaying their arrival at the villa named "La Belle Époque". "La Belle Époque" was set in a narrow cross street between rue de la Mouzaïa and rue de Bellevue, lined with small townhouses with an old-fashioned charm that made you forget you were in the heart of Paris.

Nevertheless, time was short, and the child eaters' relentless agenda would not wait for them. The chronological sequence displayed in their Bastion office was imprinted firmly on both their minds. There were only two days left to have any chance of saving Julie—a little less this late in the afternoon. Two days left to avoid having to pin up the photo of Julie's dismembered corpse wrapped in a bin bag next to the one of her smiling.

They finally arrived at the gate to Madame Rey's house, Julie's mother. They checked the number and looked in vain for a name on the letterbox. They inspected the garden over the fence: an abandoned kennel, a rubber bone lying on the lawn, a bowl filled with rainwater. They tried to spot someone inside, but the curtains were all drawn. Life had come to a standstill since Julie's disappearance.

They rang the bell and waited, hiding their nerves. How strange it was to see two *flics*, hands in their pockets, looking embarrassed, obviously reluctant to rouse the place from its slumbers. They rang the bell again. After a few minutes, the net curtain on the front door finally stirred. They could see a dull eye peering out.

Giancarlo called out to the eye, waving his police badge over the gate. It vanished, and the door opened. Julie's mum was thirty-six, but the woman who stood in the doorway looked ten years older. She unsteadily moved towards the gate dressed in a dirty pale blue bathrobe, her greasy hair matted in tangled strands.

Alex realised at once that this haggard ghost was full of anxiolytics, and she instinctively took a step back and stood behind Giancarlo. They should have warned her before coming, she thought. She could see it in those eyes that had just pulled her back. Those eyes in which you could read a terrible mixture of hope and fear. 'What have those two police officers just told me? Have they found her? Is she dead?'

Alex's stomach was in a knot. She did not know if Giancarlo had grasped her unease; he was used to leading the discussions and spontaneously spoke up to explain the purpose of their visit. The eyes immediately faded back to their resigned despondency. The gate opened, they crossed the garden and were, finally, invited into the house.

The front door opened into a small kitchen. Madame Rey went to stand at the sink and put her trembling hand on the edge of the stack of dirty dishes. She waited a few seconds before looking painfully at Giancarlo, who pulled up the screenshot from the surveillance video showing the woman from behind who had taken Julie the day she disappeared.

Madame Rey picked it up with a slow, indecisive gesture, and Alex noticed that the first thing she looked at was her daughter's face. She gently stroked it tenderly with her fingertips. Alex looked away, feeling dizzy. She asked Madame Rey's permission to look at Julie's bedroom and disappeared into the house. She climbed the spiral staircase to the first floor while Giancarlo and Madame Rey discussed the video: could she identify the lady seen from behind?

At the top of the stairs, Alex leant against the wall for a moment, just long enough to regain her composure. She had to pull herself together… for the investigation, for Giancarlo and Julie. She knew it was not too late. She could feel it. She banged her head lightly against the wall, inhaled and exhaled deeply. She opened her eyes again and realised that she was in front of the girl's room.

The door was wide open, the bed made, but you could see that someone had been lying in it. The duvet and pillowcase still bore traces of the body that had curled up under the covers and stayed there.

Alex stood for a long moment in the doorway, as if her presence would sully Julie's privacy, and now that of her mother. Her eyes swept over the small room. Despite being eleven years old, Julie was lingering in childhood, not wishing to give it up: soft toys spilling from the bed, a Lego farm, a wooden construction set, a shelf filled with children's books, small, coloured boxes, and other keepsakes. A photo in a pink frame and a book from the "Max and Lili" collection stood on the bedside table.

Attracted like a magnet by the photo in the pink frame, Alex decided to go in and grab it. It was a photo of Julie taken in a large park–presumably Buttes-Chaumont–holding a young, short-haired, cream Labrador. Alex could not take her eyes off this innocuous photo of the child with her dog. She was hypnotised by it as if the image held a coded message that she was unable to decipher.

Alex scanned every detail. Were there other people in the background? An enigmatic figure hiding behind a tree, watching his prey? Nothing like that. And yet, her instincts told her that there was something there.

Alex shrugged off the slight niggle that told her to take another look. She gently put the photo back and quietly went back downstairs, slightly annoyed at not finding anything more.

She found Giancarlo in the kitchen, a coffee in his hand. When he saw her, he shook his head discreetly to signal that Madame Rey had not recognised the woman in the photo. Inwardly Alex was incensed: this investigation was sapping them. It wasn't that they weren't making progress; they just weren't making sufficient, and, more particularly, not fast enough; a succession of clues proving incomplete, lighting the way without showing the end.

As the door closed on them, Alex took one last look inside the house through the curtains and saw Madame Rey shuffling up the spiral staircase.

They stood in the garden, motionless and dejected, unsure how they should proceed after unsuccessfully playing their last card. Alex walked into the garden, looked around again, then focused on the front of the house. She had the feeling that something was wrong, or rather something was missing, without being able to explain it.

Giancarlo watched her as her eyes went from the garden to the façade. What did she see? He tried to understand. He looked around the garden left untended since Julie's disappearance: the weeds, the dead leaves, the kennel, and the dog bowl abandoned under the lime tree. Then he looked at the front of the house, still in good condition, a bit of damp under the gutter overflowing with dead leaves. What was she looking for?

No, it was not the front of the house that Alex was eyeing. It was Julie's bedroom upstairs, which looked out onto the garden. She thought back to the photo taken in Buttes-Chaumont in its pretty pink frame on the bedside table that she had been looking at moments earlier. Something was nagging at the back of her mind. Suddenly, she realised what had been bothering her since the moment she left Julie's room.

'Giancarlo, where's the dog?'

They looked at each other and knew at the same time that they had something important in that simple question.

'Where's the dog?'

This question was the final thread that needed pulling to unravel the plot. Julie's life was hanging on it. The excitement rose like a spike of adrenalin: she had to act quickly.

The next hour went by in Alex's head in a flash: from Madame Rey, whom they got out of her missing daughter's bed for the second time, to the mothers of the other victims, whom they reached by phone shortly after leaving "La

Belle Époque".

Julie had been begging for a puppy for years. Her mum had given her a young Labrador to congratulate her for moving up to the sixth grade. It was suffering from osteomyelitis: an infection of the bone common in dogs. After many visits to the vet, several treatments with antibiotics, and a strict diet that proved ineffective, the vet recommended total rest: Julie's dog had since been in "cage therapy" on the vet's premises, reducing his activity to a minimum which would allow him to recover.

When they interviewed Gabriel's mother and the mothers of three of the other victims, they all confirmed that they had pets.

Then they asked them the name of their vet.

Alex and Giancarlo ran towards the car. Alex was the first to reach it and threw herself behind the steering wheel, unaffected by the pain in her ribs, neutralised by the fever of excitement. Giancarlo had not yet closed his door when the tyres squealed on the asphalt. He grumbled and ordered Alex to slow down to give the GPS time to locate them. He entered the address of Docteur Hugot's surgery in the 11th arrondissement as best he could. It would take them twenty-eight minutes exactly to reach their destination in normal traffic conditions.

All five victims had a pet. And in all five cases, the animals were treated by the same veterinary surgeon: Docteur Hugot.

26.

'I hadn't even opened the door, and I already knew...'

Giancarlo stared straight ahead as he told Alex about his evening the night before. They had just parked a few metres from Docteur Hugot's surgery and were starting their surveillance when Giancarlo suddenly felt the need to unload.

Busy looking for the presence of their suspect in the waiting room movements, Alex only listened distractedly. The waiting room looked directly onto the street, and despite a few posters advertising dog food, it was easy to see what was going on in there. On one side were chairs and a low table with magazines stacked on it. Opposite were shelves of pet food and pet care products. At the back was the reception desk. A young woman in her early twenties was stood behind it, engrossed in a computer screen. She was wearing a white coat; her hair was tied back in a ponytail and discreet make-up accentuated her youthful appearance.

'No noise... not a laugh, not a shout, not even a TV with the cartoon they have been watching for weeks...'

Giancarlo took a deep breath, unbuckled his seatbelt,

and sank further into his seat. Surprised by this unexpected confession, Alex turned her attention away from the waiting room to give him a long look. She knew he was having problems with his wife, but it had never occurred to her that they might separate.

Giancarlo had walked into the apartment devoid of all its familiar sounds; it gave him the impression he was invading someone else's. His eyes had fallen on an abandoned toy in the hallway; he had peered into the boys' room on the right, into Angelina's room on the left, and then a little further on into the room he shared with his wife. What he saw there—or rather, what he did not see—confirmed his hunch: his wife had left him and taken the children.

New anguish twisted Alex's stomach; she could not take her eyes off Giancarlo's closed, dark face. Giancarlo was a pillar of the team. Her pillar. The stability of his life and family life was an anchor for Alex in this world. A counterbalance to her suffering that had enabled her to keep her balance on the fragile thread of reason since those four days in hell. An abyss had just opened beneath her feet.

Unable to find the words, she was still staring at him, helpless and distressed, when suddenly Giancarlo sat up.

'Isn't that him?' he asked, placing a firm hand on Alex's arm which was still attached to the steering wheel.

She turned her head towards Docteur Hugot's office and immediately spotted the man Giancarlo was pointing out. The adrenaline flowed through her veins again; her grip tightened a little more on the wheel. And if Giancarlo's firm hand hadn't been on her arm, tacitly forbidding her to jump out of the car, she would have already been inside the office and pounced on that man. Their man.

Tall and very thin, his shoulders hunched as though apologising for his height. His face framed by short, neat, greying hair was long, with narrow eyes and an aquiline nose that unbalanced the whole. He wore the usual white coat over baggy jeans that emphasised, rather than camouflaged, his almost sickly thinness.

The vet was stood by the reception desk. He was chatting with a woman in her forties, holding a sleeping cat and smiling at him while shaking her head. He was there, a few metres away, and –if Salvac were not mistaken–Julie would still be alive.

'What do we do now?' Alex asked loudly without taking her eyes off the vet.

Giancarlo's jaw tightened as he slowly let go of Alex's arm, contemplating the best strategy: they had rushed to the vet's office when they left Julie's mum's house, convinced that they had their culprit. But the evidence was still wafer-thin and certainly insufficient to justify an arrest.

Giancarlo took his phone out of his inside pocket and called the judicial police intelligence centre. They did not need any authorisation to get the information they needed on Docteur Hugot. He mechanically ran through the usual list for the officer on the other end of the line: background, addresses, leases, property titles, personal and family, especially within a two-hundred-kilometre radius of Paris, vehicles and, specifically, utility vehicles.

'Let's keep watching for the moment,' Giancarlo replied after hanging up. We'll go and interview him at his home address when he's finished work. Then we'll see…'

Alex nodded slowly, chafing at the bit. If she had listened to herself, she would already be strangling Docteur Hugot, forcing him to spit out the address of his macabre lair to rescue Julie. Yes, she knew what she was capable of when she lost her temper: forgetting her responsibilities as a *flic*, forgetting that a *flic* did not have full powers, and there was presumption of innocence law to be respected.

She still had a shred of clarity: she should no longer trust herself, at least when it came to such decisions.

27.

'We would like to ask you some questions,' Giancarlo announced.

It was 8:16 p.m., and they had followed Docteur Hugot home once the surgery closed. He had taken payment from the last clients; his young receptionist having left at 6:00 p.m. He had taken off his white coat and hung it up in the reception area, then spent a long moment alone in his office before leaving with a satchel slung over his shoulder. He had come out of the practice, which he locked up, and found himself on the pavement. He walked briskly up towards a crossroad jammed with cars and returned home after a hard day's work, like Mister Everyone.

Alex had waited until he was far enough away to start the engine and follow him at a distance. Inwardly, she could hardly wait. The last few hours had been long, waiting in the car, watching the suspect come and go freely, while a child held somewhere was worrying about her mother and herself. She had felt the pressure building inside her. Her body was a bundle of nervous tics, which she tried to contain as best she could. She knew that Giancarlo would not hesitate to remove her from the investigation at the slightest doubt about her ability to cope. She had watched him on the sly as she drove. He was there, sitting in the car, looking towards the vet. Still, she sensed that he was elsewhere, preoccupied with something else. Which was good for her in a way—he would be less attentive to the tension building up inside her—but added to her anxiety: would he be able to intervene if she lost control?

Alex parked on a pedestrian crossing about twenty metres from the entrance to the building that Docteur Hugot had entered after a twenty-minute walk. She had listened as Giancarlo shared with her the latest information on the vet.

Docteur Hugot had owned a flat in the 13th arrondissement for nine years. By contrast, he did not enjoy any family property simply because he had no family. Docteur Hugot was nobody's child. Docteur Hugot was what is commonly called a "DDASS[37] child".

'What's this about?' he asked, looking at the police badge Giancarlo presented to him and scrutinising it.

Then he looked to check that it was Capitaine Ranieri.

'Can we come in?' insisted Giancarlo, 'It won't take long.'

Docteur Hugot seemed to hesitate and then stepped aside to leave the way clear for the two police officers. Giancarlo went in first, followed by Alex, instructed to say nothing, to do nothing but observe the scene and the suspect's reactions.

From the moment they had decided to mount the interrogation, Alex had been mentally bandaging herself, trying to control her nervous tics. The first one ran from her

---

37 Direction Départementale des Affaires Sanitaires et Sociales.

shoulder to her elbow, and the most embarrassing one slightly twisted her upper lip into a tight smile. Alex felt as if she was turning into a hunting dog, a bloodhound made to smell an item of clothing and released on a stalker's scent trail.

If Giancarlo had noticed Alex's increasing nervousness, he did not show it.

Docteur Hugot closed the door and stood by it, turned towards the two police officers. He made it obvious he did not want them hanging around too long; he was not about to offer them coffee and a friendly chat.

While Giancarlo was giving a very factual account of the context of their visit–five of the victims had pets that Docteur Hugot had treated–and asking pertinent questions–Did he remember these children? Did they come to the practice often? Were they accompanied? Had he noticed anything unusual?–Alex took stock of the situation.

The apartment was typical of the apartments built in the resolutely modernist 70s real estate frenzy: cubic, with low ceilings and a large bay window opening onto a balcony transformed into a veranda enlarging the living space. The front door led directly into the living room, which must have been the largest in the apartment. The entrance to the kitchen was visible to the right, as was a narrow passageway towards the back. The passageway had cupboards along its entire length and three doors coming off it: presumably to the bedroom, bathroom, and separate toilet. The floor had been carpeted, the plaster on the walls was slightly yellowish. The apartment was immaculately clean and spartanly decorated: no pictures on the walls, no photographs.

Docteur Hugot had no family or friends.

Alex would have liked to open the doors at the back to find out for sure. But from the moment Docteur Hugot had let them in, from the moment her foot had crossed the threshold, from the moment she had run her eyes over the room, Alex had sensed, without being able to explain it, that they would find nothing here.

Julie was not there.

Docteur Hugot was answering Giancarlo's questions dryly. Listening attentively, Alex did not perceive any nervousness or concern in either his tone of voice or expression on his face. He was mechanically impassive, perhaps due to his personal history of abuse, neglect, abandonment, and foster care. Few of the children in the DDASS were doing as well as Docteur Hugot, professionally at least.

And as she watched him, Alex thought coldly that–ironically?–Docteur Hugot was as ugly as the life he had likely experienced and had a guilty profile that was too good to be true.

This interrogation was going nowhere. Had they made another mistake?

Giancarlo ended the interview by leaving his business card with Docteur Hugot. Alex studied his face one last time: no sign, no change, no trace of relief. Total self-control.

On the doorstep, Giancarlo hesitated, then turned around and said: 'We would also like to talk to your receptionist.'

'The easiest way to do that is to come by the office tomorrow morning. She arrives at 8:00am. The first appointments don't start until 9:00am.'

Giancarlo nodded. As they walked towards the lift, Docteur Hugot added: 'But you won't learn much from this one.

She's a temp. My receptionist is on leave until the end of the month.'

They noted the name of his permanent receptionist, and the door slowly closed on them.

'Un fico secco[38],' thought Giancarlo.

Alex got behind the wheel again and, while fastening her seatbelt, thought aloud: 'Not once… not once did he look at me.'

38 A hill of beans

THE LAST BITE

28.

Alex and Giancarlo had returned to the Bastion, deserted at that hour. Neither of them had felt like going home to an empty, gloomy apartment. Alex had followed Giancarlo, who led the way with his determined step: they had gone up to the third floor via the grand staircase, then walked down the long corridor to their office. Alex had sat at the table facing the evidence board while Giancarlo stood at the window.

Alex seemed hypnotised, looking for something they had missed. Her gaze kept returning to the chronological sequence, to Julie's photo and the question mark written in red marker pen on tomorrow's date. Tomorrow... that was only a few hours away. If they went past that date without doing anything, then Julie's smiling picture would be juxtaposed with Julie's dead and dismembered one, a stinging reminder of the failure they were going through. Her stomach knotted a little more. The photo of Julie and her dog, her mother's pale blue dirty bathrobe, the bedside table and its small keepsakes, Julie's room frozen in time, danced before her eyes.

Nevertheless, they still had a few hours to go, and it was

certainly worth giving it one last shot. But Alex felt limp, unable to come up with a new avenue to explore. She glanced at Giancarlo leant against the window, his head buried in the crook of his arm, his shoulders and back rounded. He was no longer there either.

Alex looked away. They just needed a rest to get their energy back. Yes, just a rest... Then she would go over all the items on the evidence board again and find something, surely. They had a few hours ahead of them, and a few minutes of calm without thinking about anything would be enough for them to bounce back. Her eyes were closing by themselves. She didn't struggle. She just had time to rest her forehead on the table before she dozed off.

The man and the girl quietly walk along a dirt path lined by large ash trees with reddish leaves. The dog comes and goes around them, frantically wagging its tail, delighted to see its young mistress again and be able to run free without a leash around its neck.

A light breeze sways the branches spread over their heads and loosens the dead leaves in clusters, which fly away and fall lazily in the low-angled sun of an autumn afternoon.

Alex looks at Julie from afar, playing with her dog, and emotion grips her heart: Julie is there, very much alive, and happy.

Julie bends down from time to time to pick up a piece of wood, tugging on the hand firmly gripping hers a little more each time. She throws the stick to her dog, which invariably runs after it, bringing it back to her owner's feet.

The man holding Julie's hand has his back to her. He is wearing a knee-length gabardine and Doc Martens.

Alex's blood freezes in her veins.

The dog brings the stick back in its mouth and drops it too far away. Julie tugs on the hand that grips hers a little more to be able to reach it.

Masson pulls her back to him with a brutal movement, causing her to miss the piece of wood shiny with saliva by a few centimetres.

Julie looks at Masson in surprise.

'Stay close to me!' he orders in a brittle voice.

Then he smiles, revealing his carnivorous teeth.

'Alex!' shouted Giancarlo in his hoarse voice, shaking her by the shoulders.

Sat terrified in her chair, her cheeks soaked with tears, Alex screamed with her eyes wide open. When she recognised Giancarlo, when she finally realised that she was in their office and had just had a nightmare, she fell silent. She blinked, swallowed, and said nothing for several minutes. Giancarlo let her come to, still stunned by the state in which she had woken up.

'Alex, it's a woman who abducts the children. So, why not Docteur Hugot's receptionist? We're on the right track; I can feel it. We mustn't give up now… Come on, let's go. I've got her address.'

Alex slowly looked up at Giancarlo.

'Giancarlo, it's too late…' she announced in a desperate voice.

'What do you mean, it's too late?'

'Julie…' she sobbed, 'she's already dead.'

THE LAST BITE

29.

Alex had followed Giancarlo, stripped of an outcome that had become more important than her life itself and just vanished into thin air. Julie was dead, and there was nothing more to be done. She was convinced. She moved forward stiffly, like a robot, led by a distraught and nervous Giancarlo. Their hands were sweaty, and he was pulling her as best he could towards the car.

The night was cold and damp. The mist had thickened and made the ambient air opaque and dense. The sounds of the night seemed distorted, muffled.

Was she still dreaming? Was Masson going to appear before her to torture her again, to bite her, to tear her apart? To finish her off, perhaps? To finally get it over and done.

The truth had to be accepted: Giancarlo had not saved her by snatching her from Masson in extremis. He had only prolonged the agony. She retched; her stomach turned over with nothing to bring up in a spasm of helpless agony. A gaping hole had opened beneath her feet, and she was falling into a bottomless pit like Alice in Terrorland.

Nonetheless, she was still walking, her hand clenched in

Giancarlo's. He didn't let go of her until he reached the car and quickly moved to the driver's side. She stood still, exactly where he had left her, and did not move, even as he started the engine. She didn't want to get into this car. Should she run away, should she sit there on the wet pavement and wait? For what? Should she call for help? Should she cry? She felt drained, unable to make a decision... She let her mind tumble in a dizzying fall.

Giancarlo shouted at her through the car door's lowered window. He didn't care about this investigation anymore either. He was throwing himself into this last attempt in a desperate gesture, to occupy space, time, their minds, her mind which, he could see, was in the process of completely losing its grip. This investigation had acted as a negative catalyst, undermining the precarious balance that she had maintained at arm's length for seven years. And at this very moment, as he watched her when the dam seemed to have burst, all he could see was how blind he had been, how firmly he had closed his eyes to what she had become.

She stood there, ashen, and shattered. 'Give me back her caustic outlook, her arrogance, the keen eye she had,' he implored. That penetrating gaze that saw what most could not. Himself included. That strength that radiated from within her, despite herself, despite the suffering.

'Alex, get in the fucking car, *cazzo*[39]!'

He struggled with his seatbelt, which he had only just fastened, to get out of the car. He opened the door for her, sat her in the passenger seat, and buckled her in. Taking advantage of this proximity, his face a few centimetres from

---

39 Fuck!

hers, he stopped fidgeting to look into her eyes and was seized with a violent desire to give up. His judgement threatened to shatter. Alex thought it was too late, that Julie was already dead, and Alex had never been wrong.

Where were his wife, his children? The familiar sounds, smells, laughter, warmth… He closed his eyes for a moment, still leaning over Alex. He could hear her breathing, slow, disembodied.

No, he had to hold on. He had to remember why he was there. He had to remember, first and foremost, what he was: a *flic*. He had to see this investigation through to the end.

But as he slammed the door on Alex and walked around the car to get back behind the wheel, he had a feeling that they were both heading into the dark, and the outcome was uncertain.

He started the engine and then switched on the windscreen wipers. He followed them with his eyes as though bringing his blood pressure and the ferment of his ideas into line with their regular, mechanical movements. As if to hypnotise himself.

Giancarlo woke up in a stupor. How long had he been asleep?

He glanced at Alex, still inscrutable, and in a moment of clarity, he put the car in gear and headed for Créteil in the southeast of Paris.

When they reached their destination, Giancarlo switched off the engine and turned off the headlights. The car slowly ended its journey with the sound of rolling tyres on wet asphalt, coming to a stop a few metres from the house of Madame Dracques, Docteur Hugot's veterinary assistant since 18 October 2005.

Giancarlo left the radiator on to prevent the windscreen from fogging up. He had to all but lay down on the steering wheel to study even the tiniest openings in the small house where Madame Dracques lived through the windscreen.

The 60s house consisted of a ground floor and two upper floors. The façade had not aged well; long black streaks of damp were visible along the walls and gutters; large fissures cracked the left-hand side. The tiled roof was buckling in places. The front garden was overgrown with weeds, with faded flowerbeds on either side of a cement stoop covered in mold.

Alex, extremely pale, seemed to have resurfaced. Her eyes were feverish and staring at the only lighted window in the house on the first floor. It was impossible to see what was going on in there. The window covered with a thick curtain only diffused a crack of light.

Giancarlo sat up and felt Alex fidgeting in her seat. She had a slight tremor that came in regular waves.

'Alex, I'm going to go out and look around the house. You stay here. You stay here, OK? You stay here and wait for me,' he said to her, giving her arm a firm squeeze to make contact.

She slowly turned her face towards him, her eyes still feverish, but he was reassured: her eyes caught his, a sign that she was there and that she heard what he was saying. But she found it difficult to answer.

'Go, Giancarlo. I'll wait for you…' she managed to say, her voice slurred.

She slowly closed her eyelids and added as if to reassure him: 'I'm feeling better, Giancarlo, I'm going to pull myself together.'

And her mouth flashed a smile, which turned into an awkward grin.

'Go, Giancarlo,' she repeated.

Giancarlo wanted to believe it. He had to get out of that car and walk away from Alex, now a shadow of her former self and making him feel uncomfortable. He wanted to believe that by the time he slipped away, she would be her old self again, and everything would be back to normal.

He loosened his hand from her arm, and slowly got out of the car without taking his eyes off her. He was worried that this ounce of clarity that had returned to her was disappearing.

Out of the car, at last, he welcomed the biting cold and fine drizzle that enveloped him in the dead of night with relief.

Once Giancarlo had shut the car door, Alex took over surveillance of the small, lit upstairs window. She could feel a fever rising within her. She had been uncontrollably shivering ever since they had parked in the street. She suddenly remembered a session with Docteur Levine, who had advised her to choose a happy memory and try to transport herself to it, a waking dream to chase away the memories of Masson's aggression when they became too violent.

As she stared at the window, like a lighted point of recognition, she tried to focus her mind on the memory she had chosen.

The sun is just rising and setting the horizon ablaze, chasing away the blue of the night. The calm sea is gently lapping against the still black rocks of the Mediterranean.

They have turned over a small boat, which they both carry at arm's length above their heads. It is much too heavy for her; her muscles are burning as they have just picked it up. She follows her brother with difficulty as he walks towards the water's edge as though the roughness of the rocks did not exist. She can still hear her ragged breathing, which she tries as best she can to conceal. And finally, deliverance, when the boat is in the water, and only the best remains, gliding across the calm sea to that very spot where they will find rockfish for their soup. He is the one who rows while she rests and watches him, so handsome in the early morning, in the shadow of the rising sun, pulling on the oars in graceful, steady movements with his still childlike arms.

The curtain on the first floor window fluttered.

Her brother's face shattered into a thousand pieces, sucked abruptly with the boat and the sea into a hole in her memory.

A shadow had approached the window, and a hand had caught the edge of the curtain as it slowly opened.

Alex sat upright in her seat, fully concentrated. First, she saw a woman's hand, then an arm covered with a beige shawl, and finally a head almost stuck to the window looking out. What's that about, she asked herself? Had Giancarlo made a noise while inspecting the garden around the house? Or was she just looking at the sky at night?

At last, a face came into view. Alex barely had time to see it because the glass had fogged up, creating an opaque mask, and the curtain had closed immediately.

How many thousandths of a second did Alex have to

catch a glimpse of that face? And especially that hair?

She recognised her.

Even if all she had seen was taken from behind on a poor-quality video.

Her body stiffened, and she instinctively reached into her holster to make sure her SIG Sauer was there.

There was no longer any need to procrastinate.

Her own instructions forgotten, her safeguard Giancarlo's too.

Alex gently opened the car door and carefully closed it.

She walked towards the front door without making a sound.

There was no longer any doubt: it was indeed the woman who had wrapped her arms around Julie's shoulders to take her away from her mother and dog to a completely different fate.

THE LAST BITE

30.

Malik stands in front of the mirror in his shower room, which is just big enough to hold all of him. He stands upright and shirtless. He strokes his freshly shaved cheeks with his right hand, gently running it along his jawline, his chin and, finally, his upper lip, now without a trace of stubble.

Malik thinks he is handsome with particularly fine skin, clear eyes, flawless eyebrows, and very short, very black hair. Malik had not thought he was this good-looking for a long time. Usually, he barely looks at himself when he is shaving in the morning. A smug look spreads over his face as he straightens his shoulders even more to size up his stature.

Stretching his lips slightly to smile at his reflection, he sees a drop of blood beading at the corner of his mouth. And it is when he sees this dark red drop hanging from his lip that he feels the warm, slightly alkaline liquid spreading inside his mouth.

Intrigued, he brings his face closer to the mirror, curls his upper lip and with dismay sees blood on his ivory teeth. His tongue instinctively licks them, and his heart speeds up: they move, throbbing in his gums. A cold sweat runs down his back and forehead.

His heart races as he tries to test how fixed his right canine is and it sticks to his fingers.

His eyes mist over when he grasps that he is losing all his teeth, one after the other.

And as he wobbles, his legs threatening to give out from under him, the blood continues to run into the sink, spiralling down the plughole.

Malik closes his eyes tight shut, holding onto the edges of the sink with both hands, trying not to hear his teeth falling into the ceramic bowl like a shower of pea gravel.

Malik opened his eyes wide and took a deep breath, his heart still pounding. He was no longer upright but lying in a bed. He no longer tasted blood in his mouth. He flicked his tongue over his teeth: they were all still there and stuck firmly in his gums. He let his heart settle and glanced to the right, where he saw a heart monitor; he glanced to the left, where he saw an elderly lady in a white coat hanging a plastic bag containing a translucent liquid from the top of a drip stand.

Malik was no longer in his tiny shower room but a hospital room. What was he doing here? How long had he been here? He nervously searched the depths of his memory. Strange visual fragments followed one by one before his closed eyes: Alex running up the avenue, the board with the fateful date topped by a question mark written in red felt-tip pen, the flash of a camera accompanied by a snigger, Giancarlo taking him by the shoulders, a quiet lake, Commissaire Hervé leaning against his desk, a feeling of intense nervousness.

Malik opened his eyes again to find a nurse bent over him.

'Ah, I wasn't mistaken!' she exclaimed. 'You're wide awake! How do you feel?'

'What day is it?'

'Wednesday 5 December.'

Malik closed his eyes. It was two days past the date, and here he was, still confined to his hospital bed. Where were they? Had they found the child? Had they found her alive?

'I'll go and get the intern right away...' the nurse whispered.

And she left without waiting.

Malik had just come out of his enforced sleep. A week had passed since the medical team at the Hôpital Pasteur in the 4th arrondissement had put him into an induced coma.

Nurses had been with him most of the morning, and all the commotion had given him a headache. Malik had insisted that they put his headboard straight. He wanted to get out of this room, out of this hospital, back on the street. But his body was incapable. He could feel it. All his limbs were numb, and he began to feel generalised pain despite the high dose of painkillers. Had his father and mother been notified? Had the police, his team been notified? He was told yes, but it was not yet time for visitors. Then the commotion stopped, his room emptied, and Malik was finally alone, with nothing but the cardiac monitor's throbbing beep and his migraine for company.

He was dozing when he heard the handle turn. The door to his room opened, and he heard muffled words: 'He's still fragile, Capitaine. No more than ten minutes, are we agreed?'

Malik's heart leapt in his chest at the word "Capitaine". Was it Alex? Giancarlo? What had happened? His whole being grew impatient as the door finally opened. He recognised the hand on the handle attached to an arm in worn black leather in a split second. Then all of Giancarlo filled the doorway. Everything about him said bad news: his slumped shoulders, his weary eyes. There was nothing left to hope for: the game was up, and they had lost.

Giancarlo entered the room and closed the door behind him.

'How do you feel?' he asked as he walked to the window.

Malik did not answer. It did not matter; he knew that the question was only rhetorical. Giancarlo was composing himself before delivering the bad news; he just needed more time. Malik heard him sigh.

'We screwed up,' Giancarlo announced abruptly without turning around.

Where's Alex?'

Giancarlo did not answer clearly, mumbling a few words in Italian that Malik could not make out.

'Where's Alex, Giancarlo?'

Giancarlo turned to face him. Malik looked him straight in the eye, his gaze resolute. He would not give up.

'Where's Alex, Giancarlo?' he repeated, stressing each syllable.

'I had no choice,' said Giancarlo.

31.

Giancarlo let the rain slide over him and crossed the street. As he walked along the cypress hedges that surrounded Madame Dracques' house, he looked for a way into the garden without being seen. He pushed aside a few branches here and there, hoping to find a gap in the wire fence. The house was adjacent to others, so Giancarlo had to jog to the end of the street and take a side street to get into the backyard. It covered an area of around a hundred square metres and was littered with broken pots overflowing with soil, dried out plants, and a rusting old swing seat. There was no garage, so there was a good chance that the killer had parked his vehicle on the street. He quickly inspected the cars lined up along the pavement for about fifty metres without finding anything conclusive: no utility vehicle or anything that might be considered suspicious.

He then returned to the back of the house and carefully examined the façade. He noticed a small window from which a thin halo of light was shining. So, the house had a cellar, and at that very moment, someone was in it. Giancarlo stiffened: that cellar, that light... If they were right, if that house did indeed belong to the killer, then maybe Julie was in that cellar right now. His hands clenched the fence and shook it violently as if he could have forcibly torn it down to make a rush at this cellar. Helplessly, he let out a furious groan. Pull yourself together, move fast, go back to the car, warn Alex, get inside no matter what, case of force majeure. Giancarlo let go of the fence and started to run flat out, and as he was coming back to the gate to the house, he heard a gunshot.

Corre, coglione, corre[40].

Giancarlo slipped on the first front step and fell flat on his face in front of the front door. When he stood up, he saw that it had been broken open and pieces of glass were scattered on the hall floor. He had just enough time to spot a trail of blood and a body slumped at the bottom of the staircase before being deafened by the blast of eleven shots.

Twelve in total.

A SIG Sauer had just emptied its magazine in a matter of seconds.

---

40 *Run, arsehole, run.*

32.

Alex headed for the front door. Her boots sank into the gravel crunching under her feet. She pressed the handle: the door was locked. The antiqued wood door was glazed from the handle to the top, protected by wave-shaped wrought-iron bars spaced about ten centimetres apart and studded with small, chiselled leaves. Alex pressed her face as close as she could, resting her cheeks and forehead against the cold, rough bars.

Her hair stuck to her forehead and dripped down over her eyes. She tilted her head back, blew out a deep breath to calm her racing heart. She wiped her face with trembling hands and pulled her hair back. She rested her face again against the bars. The hall was in darkness, but she managed to make out a threadbare carpet on the floor, a small chest topped by a large, heavily pitted mirror and a corridor running into even denser darkness at the back. To the left, a staircase led up to the first floor, dimly lit, undoubtedly by the room in which she had just seen the woman in the video.

Julie.

Forgetting the door was locked, Alex pressed the

handle and pushed her whole body against it to get to the light like an insect attracted to a neon sign.

Julie, was she up there? Was she alive? Had she been mistaken? A fragile ray of hope lit up in her heart.

Alex jumped and was hit full force by a jolt of adrenaline: a shadow was moving upstairs. She checked the space between two of the bars and broke the window with an elbow. She put her hand through the gap, ignoring the shards of glass that tore her skin, and slipped her arm inside; she felt for the lock, found the key, and turned it. She heard the lock click. She withdrew her arm without taking her eyes off the staircase where the shadow was still moving. She opened the door wide, took out her SIG Sauer and went into the house.

With the sound of hurried footsteps, a woman ran down the stairs, her face disfigured by fear. She turned her head towards the end of the ground floor corridor. Alex saw her throat swell with a cry, her mouth opening to let it out. She had already cocked the SIG Sauer at the end of her outstretched arm, and the throat burst into a geyser of blood before the cry could escape. The cry became a gurgle, and the woman's lifeless body collapsed, eyes bulging, and tumbled to the bottom of the stairs, leaving a dark red trail behind.

The explosion had sounded like a thunderclap ripping through the silence of the night. In a split second, Alex saw the movement of the woman's head again, just before she died. Instinctively she looked in the same direction: there was a door along the wall to her right. She was in front of it in a few steps and shattered the handle with a forceful kick. The door opened wide, slamming against the wall. Alex bolted down the narrow staircase, guided by a strip of light at the bottom. Driven by rage, Alex was no longer thinking.

It was then that she had a flashback.

A rapid flashback, so real it stopped her dead in her tracks: Masson standing in front of her with a smile across his face.

She squinted and wiped her forehead, wet not with rain but with sweat. Was it a fever? Was it fear? Was it fear of this bloodthirsty ghost looming there in front of her? She swallowed her saliva and jumped again. With a kick, she knocked down a second door.

A bright white light blinded her.

She blinked several times. When she could open her eyes again, she saw a man of about sixty years old, cornered against the back wall. She immediately aimed her gun at him. He was short—no more than six feet tall—and stocky. He was wearing a blood-stained undershirt. Old, dried bloodstains in places. Large splashes of fresh, wet blood across his torso as if lashed by several streams of it. His wild eyes overcome with fear were hidden behind transparent goggles, also covered in bloodstains. Alex's gaze shifted to his rubber-gloved hands. His left hand twitching nervously held a long, sharp steel knife dripping with blood.

Alex closed her eyes and took in a large gulp of air laden with the acrid smell of blood and the stench of the cellar. As she opened them again, her heart sank: the man was gone. In front of her stood a fierce-looking Masson, his smile revealing his teeth and blood-stained mouth. He parted his lips and spat a piece of flesh into his hand. Slowly looking up at her, he stuck out his sharp tongue to lick his lips with relish.

'It's my little relic,' he breathed, slipping the piece of

flesh into the right-hand pocket of his gabardine.

She then felt a severe pain between her thighs: the phantom appendage. The pain was so searing that she bent double and fell to her knees.

And he disappeared, leaving her trembling, her heart pounding in her chest.

While holding the man in front of her at gunpoint, she took a quick look around the cellar: to her right was a table covered with a faded oilcloth on which lay a baseball bat and knives of various sizes, a small axe, and a roll of bin bags.

Where was she? Everything was confused in her mind… Masson… Julie… But where was Giancarlo? Michel… Yes, sat down in front of the TV at Michel's feet, not looking at the photo frame on the pedestal table. Why this photo? Of Pauline, who is not your daughter. Just there with her innocent smile to send you back to your guilt for never having managed to find her.

Finally, Alex turned her head to the left and implored all the gods she had never believed in. She was imploring with all her might when she spotted Julie's still body laid out on a thick wooden board. She recognised her hair, her round face, her snub nose. The child was lying there on an adapted butcher's block; a gutter dug into the wood, a basin filled with blood sat beneath it. At the bottom of Julie's neck, a wound ten centimetres long, partially open, blood still dripping from it. Alex looked away, unable to face the rest.

She stared straight into the eyes of the man three metres away from her, stunned like a wild animal caught in the headlights. The hair was greasy and sparse, the body muscular but flabby looking. Faded tattoos on his torso poked out above his undershirt and were on his arms too. He stood there in front of her, and he was the one who was afraid.

Alex's heart continued beating wildly. The bubbling inside her was rising. She could feel the flow of her blood imploding in every part of her body, in her skull, swirling, washing away what little sanity she had left, like a river in full flood.

It had to stop. She had reached the end of all that she could bear. She closed her eyes. How could she resist this dull, wild, indomitable impulse rising inside her? Giancarlo, she thought, or rather, she called in her heart like the last prayer.

Giancarlo.

She reopened her eyes. Masson was stood in front of her again, his expression stern. He took the small piece of flesh out of his right-hand pocket and began to suck on it. Then he spat it out with a grimace of disgust and said coldly: 'I'm returning it to you after all. You're worthless!'

Alex gasped. A spasm twisted her forward and made her open her mouth to vomit air. What was happening to her? Where was she?

Then, with a final effort, she straightened up and opened her eyes wide to find the butcher staring at her in amazement. She adjusted and aimed her arm extended by a SIG Sauer.

She pulled the trigger.

Again.

And again.

Without being sure who she had just shot down, Masson or the butcher.

THE LAST BITE

33.

Giancarlo found Alex kneeling in the cellar, still pulling the trigger even though she had long since emptied the magazine. He sat her down at the bottom of the stairs where she stood, and gently took the gun out of her hand.

'É tutto finito[41], it's over…'

He hugged and cuddled her like a child. He felt her relax bit by bit, her breathing becoming calmer. They stayed like that for quite a while, exhausted. Giancarlo looked around, taking in the crime scene, every detail. He understood what had happened a few minutes before his arrival and asked no questions. Alex's hunch had been the right one: Julie was probably already dead when they left the Bastion. Their only reward was there in front of their eyes: slammed against the wall by the force of eleven bullets, he had slowly slid to the ground, leaving a dark red trail behind him. In a state of near-insanity, Alex had shown great clarity about her target. Giancarlo could only guess at the order in which she had fired. The bullets had taken everything: the eyes and the whole upper part of the head, the

41 It's all over

heart, and finally the crotch, of which there was nothing left, a gaping red hole, flesh shredded to the pubis.

The butcher could no longer hurt anyone.

Now it was time to get a grip and think about a strategy: Alex had broken into a house without a warrant and executed two people at point-blank range, one of whom was unarmed and the second blown to bits. The IGPN[42] would come down on them like a ton of hot bricks and open an investigation, the outcome of which was a forgone conclusion.

Alex was not moving and trying to regain her composure little by little. The force of the adrenaline rush had drained her last strength. She could not take her eyes off Julie. She looked at her so intensely that for a moment, it seemed that the girl's chest rose slightly as if life was returning now that her torturer was dead.

She wished she could have spoken to Giancarlo, but nothing came out. Far be it from her to apologise. She had no regrets about what had just happened, even if she was aware that she was no longer herself and that an unsuspected force had taken control. She, alone, would assume responsibility for her actions, even if it meant paying the consequences. No, she wasn't afraid of that. Her only regret was being unable to save Julie. Even if she knew that she had just saved future victims by finishing off the killer today.

Nonetheless, even if she managed to regain her composure, she realised that the leaden blanket she wore over her heart was still there, no more and no less heavy. What was it going to take to make this pressure go away?

42 Inspection Générale de la Police Nationale (General Inspectorate of the National Police)

Alex was not fooled and knew Giancarlo inside out. She knew he was thinking about it, about the IGPN, about finding a way to spare her—again.

They stood together in silence, each preoccupied with their own worries.

Giancarlo made the first move. His thoughts were clear now. He knew it would be hard for Alex, but after considering all the possibilities, he could see no other solution than the one he had just decided upon.

'Come on, Alex. Let's get out of here. I can't stand this place any longer.'

He struggled to move her body up the cramped stairs. Alex raised her face to him, and for a few seconds, their eyes met. He finally saw her with her hair in disarray, stuck to her forehead by sweat, her cheeks inflamed, and her eyes still reddened. As for Alex, she understood from Giancarlo's eyes and his clenched jaw that the resolution he had just made was costing him. And her stomach contracted. He wasn't angry with her, she could feel it, but he had just made a difficult decision.

They climbed the stairs and stepped out of the front door. They welcomed the cold and wetness of the rain with relief. But no sooner had they stepped outside than they heard sirens in the distance. The neighbours had alerted the emergency services.

'Alex?'

Alex turned and faced Giancarlo.

'Do you trust me?'

She swallowed and nodded, despite her doubts.

'Let me handle it then. Wait for me here.'

Alex sat down on the bottom step and pulled both sides

of her jacket tightly together to protect herself from the cold that had just bitten her. She accepted that she must now abandon herself to her fate. And even though deep down she knew that nothing good was going to happen to her, she convinced herself that Giancarlo would do his best.

The sound of sirens grew louder. The blue and red of the flashing lights were soon upon them, bringing them back to reality.

She watched Giancarlo walk away from her to meet the police officers who had just got out of the first vehicle. He took his badge out of the inside pocket of his jacket. The police officers listened attentively. Giancarlo immediately commanded respect as usual, and it wasn't just a matter of his badge. Giancarlo turned several times towards the house, the police officers followed his gaze systematically, nodding from time to time. One of them asked a few questions before finally returning to the service vehicle and grabbing the radio microphone. She saw Giancarlo sigh and turn towards her. He nodded, inviting her to join him. Alex stood up painfully as if her body was aching.

'Let's go.'

'Where are we going?' she managed to articulate.

'I'll tell you in the car.'

He took her arm firmly, and she obediently followed him. The police officer had just put the microphone down and was trotting back towards them. She saw the knowing look he exchanged with Giancarlo.

Giancarlo walked Alex to the passenger side. He let her get in and slammed the door shut. She watched him walk back around the car. She couldn't take her eyes off him, waiting for an answer to her question. Then the driver's door opened, and Giancarlo got in. He turned the key in the ignition, and the engine purred. He put the car into reverse, and as he turned to check that the road was clear, his arm came to rest on Alex's seat.

'I'm taking you to Sainte-Anne[43],' he announced.

'Don't do this, Giancarlo… please,' she pleaded.

'If I don't do this, Alex, it's the IGPN on my back… and then prison…'

'We're not finished,' she huffed.

'What do you mean?'

'The vet… the vet is behind it, I'm sure.'

Giancarlo was speechless.

'He chooses them. I can feel it.'

Giancarlo's eyes went from the road to Alex, not knowing what to believe. The events of the last few hours had mentally exhausted him. He was unable to think. The only thing he knew was that he had to get her to safety.

'We'll talk about this later, Alex. You need to rest and digest everything that has just happened.'

Alex shook her head slowly.

'I won't survive if I'm committed…' and her voice broke into a sob.

Giancarlo bit the inside of his cheek to stop himself from breaking down. Their world was crumbling… swept away like raindrops on the windscreen with a wiper blade. He knew at that very moment that even if it were the best solution for Alex, this decision would change their relationship forever.

---

43 Centre Hospitalier Sainte-Anne, a psychiatric hospital in Paris

THE LAST BITE

34.

Michel stood staring into the distance for a long time after Giancarlo's departure. He had hesitated before opening the front door. Yes, yes, Giancarlo. He remembered him, but Michel had lost the habit of visitors. Why was he there? Why wasn't Alex with him? All this made him extremely nervous. He swayed from one foot to the other a few steps from the front door. Giancarlo insisted. It was about Alex. He was going to have to let him in. He didn't want to hear about *flics* anymore, but Alex was different. She was just like his own kid. The police force was over for him even though he had been part of this big family for a long time. Not that he had had a hard time of it or any more sordid cases than his colleagues. He had had his share like all the others. But he had been left with the bitter taste of defeat, of unfinished business. A single investigation he had not managed to complete. It floated around him like an overcoat that is too large, too long, that lurks and becomes threadbare over the years but never stops scratching your skin. After devoting his whole life to the police, sacrificing a married life and family life that had never been... These days, he did not want to hear any more about it. He wanted to be left alone. He had given enough.

And when you give everything and get nothing in return, you simply hang your hat and let yourself shrivel up, inside and out. Michel had become old overnight. Since the first day of his retirement, his life had consisted of this flat, "his" TV, Alex's visits, and the photo of a twelve-year-old child with long hair and a happy looking face.

His trembling hand reached for the chain. Giancarlo's tone had become more urgent. He could feel the tension, the Italian accent taking over, making the word pebbles roll a little more. And then he had told him it was about Alex. What had happened to her? Was it something serious?

Worried, he finally undid the chain and opened the door. He immediately heard Giancarlo's sigh, a sigh of relief.

'Michel, you remember me…'

'What happened to her?' Michel cut him off without inviting him in.

Giancarlo had just come back from the hospital and would have to face a damning look for the second time when he announced what he had just done.

After listening to him, Michel closed the door on Giancarlo. He put the chain back and returned to the living room and his armchair in front of the TV. But he could no longer see the picture or hear the sound. His eyes immediately went to Pauline's portrait. Then he looked down at his hands: a few liver spots, crumpled skin, and a slight tremor. He put his fingers together clumsily. He sank into the chair, took a deep breath, and fell asleep despite himself.

Michel walks painfully along the pavement. Blazing

sunshine and the heat make him sweat profusely. His feet drag on the grit littering the tarmac. With his hand to his visor to protect himself from the bright light this unusually hot late afternoon, he sees the bus shelter, isolated on this long country road, about a hundred metres from him. Michel walks with difficulty: his feet sticking to the heat-melted tarmac.

He looks around and recognises the "Les Alouettes" residential area.

Yes, it had been an unusually hot day, and Pauline was on her way to the local swimming pool, where she took part in almost daily training sessions. A few houses around but empty of their residents who were still at work. No witnesses.

Michel takes a few steps to the side, and that's when he sees her. Alone, sitting on the bus shelter bench, wearing a little red dress, headphones in her ears, holding her backpack against her chest like a prized possession.

Michel checks the time on his watch. 4:36 p.m. He's ecstatic: she's there, within easy reach!

She is *still* there.

He hears a roar in the distance and recognises the dispatch rider who was the last person to see Pauline alive at her bus shelter at exactly 4:38 p.m.

'I'm sure of it,' the rider chanted, 'because when I saw her, I checked the time on the dashboard by reflex, and it said 4:38 p.m.'

Michel starts to run, two minutes to catch up with her before she vanishes without a trace. Taken aback, he realises that he is treading water, his legs moving in a vacuum. He looks at his watch again: 4:37 p.m.

'Pauline! Pauline!' he shouts.

Then it was no longer his body treading water but the bus shelter moving away at a dizzying speed: two hundred metres, five hundred metres, one kilometre, and the bus shelter disappears out of sight in a few seconds.

Everything freezes.

Michel does not move an inch.

Suddenly, the bus shelter reappears, returns at full speed, and comes to an abrupt halt about ten metres away.

It is empty.

Michel consults his watch: it is 4:39 p.m.

Pauline has disappeared.

When Michel woke up, he was disoriented, and it took him a while to come to his senses. Alex... Alex was in Sainte-Anne. He didn't blame Giancarlo. Just because you've withdrawn from the world and shrivelled up inside doesn't mean you don't pay attention to anything. He had seen that Alex was not well since the Masson affair. He had not known any more about it than what he had seen on the news. She had come back to visit him soon enough, as usual, as if nothing had changed, as if nothing should change. And he had not asked, had not demanded to know. He had understood that she did not want to and that if she came here, it was to regain some anonymity, to step into a bubble because time had stopped at Michel's a long time ago.

And it was good for him not to have to talk about it, not to have to console her. He did not know how! He had never known how. Yet, he looked on her as his child, even if he was not good at demonstrating affection.

Yes, he had seen that she was not well, but she was a strong girl. He had seen that when they worked together after she had just joined the police force. She was bright, cheeky, and brilliant. And already such a *flic* at heart. She would get used to it.

And then, of course, he had noticed in the last few months that she was not very fat. That she was having difficulty swallowing soup, that she didn't want to eat.

He fumbled in the folds of the armchair for the TV remote and turned it off. He got up and walked over to the window to look down on the bustling weekday street. How long had it been since he had been out? He barely used the phone. He turned the handle and had to force it a little. The window creaked open. Immediately he was overcome by the noise and the smell. He closed his eyes but held on. He just had to get used to it again. He could do it. He had to. He reopened his eyes and looked at the city below him until the feeling of panic subsided. Then he closed the window again, with relief and determination: he had to. He just had a phone call to make.

What a strange feeling when he hung up. Talking to somebody again, finding an old friend, not being embarrassed by trivial phrases or common reproaches.

An hour after saying goodbye to Capitaine Bernard, Michel carefully descended the stairs and finally found himself in the street. He offered his face to the falling drizzle and squinted his eyes like a condemned man coming out of his cell after several years of confinement and finding the light of day. More than the noise, he was besieged by the nauseating city smells. He sniffed the air, the exhaust pipe fumes, the smell of garbage and stale piss.

The smells he recognised so well brought back to him the sensations of old memories, of a life that had been and was no longer him, just as effectively as a madeleine dunked in tea.

The sound of a horn startled him. He hesitated for a few seconds and then turned left with a determined step.

35.

She had closed her eyes and offered her face to the icy drizzle. Sitting on a bench in the tree-lined grounds of the main pavilion at the Hôpital Saint-Anne, Alex let time pass. It seemed to have stood still since Giancarlo had abandoned her there. There was no resentment, no anger. Her thoughts sank softly into her anxiolytic-soaked brain. Through her eyelids, she could see patches of light sweep across her face whenever the leaves of the elm tree she was sat under rustled.

How long had she been locked up here? She no longer knew. Time had distended and retracted at the same time. And although still punctuated with day and night and a well-defined schedule, she had lost all her bearings. How long had she been on this bench? Without a watch or a phone? It was impossible to say. She seemed to be asking the question more as a matter of form. Deep down inside, she didn't care anymore.

She opened her eyelids and studied her feet for a moment. Her shoes, to be more precise. Without their laces. Removed when she was admitted. She wanted to smile, but the bottom of her face was completely numb. She finally looked down at her hand resting beside her leg on the cracked wood of the bench. She could barely feel the roughness of the wood under her fingers. She scratched the faded varnish with the tip of her fingernail.

'They took my baby, you know. They took it away from me… I don't know what they did with it… It's my baby, and they took it away from me… Why did they take it away from me?… My baby, you know… Well, they took it away from me…'

Alex looked up at the woman stood in front of her, slightly stooped; her hair was an unsavoury yellow, rough, and left uncombed for quite a while. Marguerite was her roommate. So, Alex ran into her several times a day and often ate with her. Marguerite always talked to her about her baby. And nothing could be done about it: whether you listened to her, pitied her, or ignored her, Marguerite tirelessly continued her lament about the baby. Had this baby ever existed?

'Marguerite, you're annoying me!' shouted Alex. 'Go away!'

Marguerite remained silent but did not budge an inch.

'Get out of my way,' Alex wanted to shout, but it was a hoarse, hollow cry that came out of her mouth.

Marguerite turned on her heels and marched away, vexed.

Alex closed her eyes again and let herself be drawn gently into the chemical languor that flowed through her veins and diffused into every cell of her mind and body. No more good, no more bad. What does Julie's death matter, what does this unfinished investigation matter, which swept away a part of its truth with the death of two protagonists? What about Giancarlo? What about the bites of the past?

Her fingernail continued to scrape away the flaking varnish, and she was lulled by the light scraping of her fingernail on the wood when she felt a hand rest on her shoulder: a gentle touch, an uncertain pressure.

'How are you doing, pet?'

Alex flinched when she recognised the voice. She slowly turned her face towards Michel's who was staring at her intently.

'Can you make a bit of space for me? I'm getting old. And this whole thing has been going round and round in my head for the last few days! But you, how're you doing, eh?' said Michel, sitting down next to her.

He patted her thigh affectionately.

'I can hardly speak…,' she managed to articulate with considerable effort.

Michel was still watching her very carefully. She saw concern in his eyes.

She swallowed and added: 'But it's OK…'

Michel left his hand on her thigh and gave it a gentle squeeze.

'But can you walk?' he asked her when he was thinking "run".

Alex nodded, making a gesture with her hand to indicate her jaw and make it clear that this ankylosis affected only her ability to talk.

'Yes, yes, I can see that it's your jaw… it seems numb… good, good.'

He looked around as though to make sure no one was watching them. Alex watched him, increasingly intrigued by his demeanour. She didn't quite understand what was going on. Michel, here, away from home, in the Hôpital

Sainte-Anne… She had not had visitors until now. She even thought she was forbidden to have any.

'How… why are you here?' she murmured, wondering if she was dreaming.

Michel looked at her intensely and, with a voice full of gravity, replied: 'A door must be closed.'

Alex swallowed hard. She understood without understanding. She wasn't sure if her brain was still functioning normally. Was this sentence supposed to be crystal clear? But Michel did not give her time to think.

'Oh, if you only knew! Me, who didn't talk to anyone, and who didn't go out anymore… All I had to do to be able to see you! But after all these years, I still have good contacts…' he answered almost joyfully, patting Alex's thigh again as if she were an old friend that it was a pleasure to meet again, and you could tell them a good joke. Then, suddenly finding his seriousness, he added: 'You could drive, couldn't you?'

And this question was more an expression of hope than a genuine inquiry. Michel brought his face close to hers. He was trying to pierce the depths of her eyes to find the answer to his question. Alex did not blink and saw Michel's pupils dilate as he concentrated.

She nodded slowly. This story was becoming so strange that she was still wondering if it was real. She could smell Michel's smell, that mixture of mustiness and dust. She could feel the weight of his hand on her thigh.

'Well, well…' continued Michel.

And he checked again that they were alone. A couple of people walked along a path running alongside the pavilion into the woods about twenty metres from them. A little closer, but at a reasonable distance, Marguerite was in deep conversation with a patient on the pavilion porch, probably telling the story of her baby for the umpteenth time.

Michel, at the peak of his nervousness, turned abruptly to Alex.

'We'll have to be quick... I couldn't bring anything with me... because of the frisking, do you see? So... Listen to me carefully... You can give me some of your attention, can't you? You'll remember what I told you, right?'

Alex nodded again, although she was unconvinced. Since her internment, her brain was completely numb and struggling to hold on to the real world around her. Concentrating on Michel's words required a superhuman effort. She was completely stunned by what was happening. Michel here? Had Michel come to help her? After so many years of abandoning his life, himself, sleepy sea no longer waiting for a tide, a mist on dry land.

Michel nervously patted Alex's thigh to get her attention, and as though to reassure himself.

'Well, it's quite simple... I didn't think you'd be this numb... but never mind... No, no, I'm confident you'll manage! But you'll need to be quick... You don't have much time... time for the visit. Listen to me carefully now.'

Alex opened her eyes as if to listen better. She fastened her gaze on Michel's lips: words here, words there, which must have formed a whole. The flood engulfed her. She listened, putting things in order, assimilating the information he was giving her.

Michel had not spoken for a few seconds already, but he continued to make a strange movement with his mouth, dry from too much talking. So many words in a few minutes, perhaps many more than in the last ten years. Michel was looking at her, his pupils agitated.

After many detours in her brain, the words and then the sentences finally made sense. Alex mused that Michel belonged in Hôpital Sainte-Anne as much as she did and that she would never, ever, manage to do a quarter of what he was asking of her.

36.

Alex stood up in slow motion. Behind her, Michel was walking up the slope towards the pavilion exit with some difficulty. She looked straight ahead: one foot in front of the other, one foot after the other. Time was pressing, but her body could give her no more. Her feet were sinking into the grass, getting stuck in it like mud. Carrying her body forward. Accelerating, because she needed to run. Heading to the right towards the small copse that led to the perimeter wall. She stumbled and fell flat on her face. Her body was unresponsive.

She sat up as best she could. 'Move, Alex, react!' she railed at herself. She set off again, staring at her goal: the perimeter wall. She ran awkwardly, but she ran, concentrating on every step, every movement. She reached the wall in a few seconds.

'You'll find a way to get over it...' Michel had said.

As she sensed the commotion of hospital staff where she had left a bench empty, she studied the four-metre-high wall with a look of panic. Built of ashlar, it offered some rough edges to climb up it. Wrought-iron spikes about thirty centimetres tall crowned it. She looked around… Perhaps a tree? Easier to climb and would enable her to jump over the wall? But she was entirely surrounded by huge old elms whose first branches were out of reach, and trunks had nowhere to grip.

So, she attacked the wall: she found one and then two holds where she could wedge her hands and then her feet to climb a metre but fell on the third. Searing pain burned her forehead, and she felt a hot, thick liquid running down her face. She wiped it and realised it was blood. She saw a trail of blood on the wall where she had fallen, where she had skinned her forehead.

She stood up and moved back a few feet. She caught her breath and closed her eyes to concentrate. She wanted to feel all the energy through her body, to be able to control it better and guide it towards her goal. She opened her eyes again and spotted some holds higher up on the wall. She took a run-up, put her weight on her right foot at the last moment and leapt as high up as she could, her feet flat, using her body weight to stay balanced against the wall. Her hands found the rough edges she had spotted.

Her balance was precarious. Her fingers were numb. She had to secure her feet to be able to climb and reach the top of the wall. She tapped her right foot and finally found a notch where she could stick the tip of her shoe. But she couldn't find one for her left foot; her boot was too wide. She shook her leg, and the shoe, already untied, fell into the grass below. She finally managed to scramble up and get to the top. She pulled herself up to the wrought-iron spikes by the strength of her arms. She took a quick look at the surveillance camera and, with great difficulty, stepped over the crown of spikes to find herself precariously balanced on the street side. She heard the rumblings getting closer: she had little time left before the men in white coats would be upon her, and she would have no chance of escaping in her state.

She took a deep breath and hung herself down the other side by her arms, blocking out the pain of her bleeding forehead and fingertips grazed on the stones. She jumped and collapsed on the pavement. She leaned against the wall as best she could to regain her composure and mopped her eyes with the back of her sleeve while looking for Michel's car.

When she finally spotted the old Citroën AX, she wondered if it really truly was red or if it was her blood running over her eyes adding a colour filter to everything she saw.

Alex got into the car, the door of which had been left unlocked. She found the keys in the ignition. The car sped off and headed straight for Fleury-Mérogis prison.

A door had to be closed.

She parked on the side of the road just before the entrance to the car park. She searched the trunk and found the pack and a bottle of mineral water.

Thirsty, she took long sips of water and washed her face. Then she threw the empty bottle into the ditch.

She put on the uniform, contorting herself in the back seat, and put on a pair of ranger boots. She got out of the car and buckled the slightly worn black leather belt, to which she attached the truncheon, handcuffs, pepper spray, and radio. She checked the SIG Sauer was loaded and inserted it into its holster. When she returned to the driver's seat, she took one last look in the rear-view mirror. She tidied her hair and adjusted the cap low enough over her eyes.

She restarted the car and passed the checkpoint using the badge she found in her pack. Finally, she parked in the employees' car park and switched off the engine.

And as she caught her breath, a ray of sunlight broke through the cloud ceiling and briefly lit the way to the service door.

No one was surprised that the young trainee had already arrived at the admissions office in her uniform. It would be explained to her later that the wardens had a cloakroom. It enabled them to come and go in civilian clothes and leave the prison world stench behind them.

A few quick hellos, then Alex was introduced to her mentor. Capitaine Bernard, a massive, paunchy-looking man with an honest face, eyeing Alex while sipping his coffee.

'Michel is an old friend of mine,' he said finally, placing his cup on the windowsill overlooking the building's inner courtyard.

He pulled a badge from his right front pocket and placed it carefully next to the cup while giving Alex a knowing look.

'Come on, we haven't got a minute to lose…,' he began, but he didn't have time to finish his sentence.

The truncheon hit him with full force on the chin. He instantly lost consciousness and fell heavily on the restroom floor.

Alex followed the cap as it rolled across the floor and ended up at the foot of the coffee machine.

Capitaine Bernard's chin was beginning to turn red and would soon turn black: indisputable proof of the aggression to which he had just fallen victim and, therefore, of his innocence in what was to follow.

Alex put the truncheon back on her belt and retrieved the badge that would give her access to the top floor of the building. The high-security section of the Violent Offender Unit was there.

THE LAST BITE

37.

Alex stood in front of the door to cell E05. Time was pressing; Capitaine Bernard's inanimate body could be discovered at any moment. Nonetheless, Alex stood motionless in front of the door, her heart beating wildly. The effect of the anxiolytics was beginning to wear off. She may have been functioning like an automaton until now, carrying out a precise list of instructions at the beginning of the end, but she could not hold back the flood of emotions that was pouring into her.

The dam built up over so many years was threatening to break. Long since cracked, she had been able to create an illusion in the minds of others and maintain a semblance of normality. But it did not protect her from the trauma that was slowly destroying her.

For seven years, she had been living in hell, wishing she had died that day when Giancarlo found her and managed to stop Masson.

Seven years of being unable to stand her body, unable to face her reflection in the mirror, suffering from wounds only superficially healed, from the burning pus of her infected soul.

Michel had understood that a line had been crossed; that the dam was much more than cracked today; that her suffering had prevailed for several days and devoured the remains of appearances, of tangible, of reasonable, of what is good, what is right.

With the badge in her hand, she had only one move to make to open that door, but her hand still hovered.

He was there, in that cell. What had he been doing for seven years? What was he thinking? Was he reliving torturing his victims for pleasure? Or perhaps torturing her? What was he dreaming about at night or during the day, his eyes lost during his long moments of solitude, locked up between the four walls of this few square metre cell?

The executioner and the victim lived the same seconds, the same minutes, the same hours, the same days, the same nights in parallel. The executioner in unceasingly renewed pleasure and the victim in self-destructive suffering.

Could she end this torture by killing her tormentor? Would removing him free her from the invisible bond that prevented her from forgetting? Did knowing that she was alive sustain her victimhood? With the executioner dead, would the bites finally heal?

'A door must be closed', Michel had told her.

Would killing him close the door on the past?

Kill him to save herself, thought Michel.

Despite everything, despite who she was, what she believed in and what she represented as a *flic*. What was the point anyway? In the last few days, she had already crossed the boundaries of the law.

Alex took a deep breath, refocused her mind. The goal was simple. She must concentrate on each step, as she had done to get to this point: one after the other. The dam had to hold.

She stuck the badge against the electronic box and heard the lock click.

Inside, the prisoner lying on his bed, his head resting on his folded arm, looked up from his book, surprised at this unexpected visit. The door opened; the guard entered the cell. Two things struck him: firstly, it was not Capitaine Bernard but a woman, and secondly, she had her service weapon in her hand.

Masson recognised her immediately when she removed her cap and smiled spontaneously as if the visitor was an old friend. He looked at her eyes, her mouth into which he had so tenderly sunk his teeth until he tasted the warmth of her flesh and blood. She had lost several kilos, but it was her. She was finally coming back to him. Because she was his, she bore his indelible bites all over her body.

Alex saw Masson's smile spread across his lips, revealing his canines that had so often planted themselves in her body, biting, tearing, wrenching too. An intense pain ran through her from her mouth to her mutilated genitals, as if each scar was splitting open in turn, leaving the flesh raw. A dazzling flash of light froze her to the spot, like a fracture of time brutally opening onto the past: Masson was standing up, his eyes misty with pleasure, his mouth dripping with blood, looking at her lovingly as she moaned, stunned by the searing pain of the bite.

"You belong to me now and forever. This mark is my seal," he whispered.

Alex approached the bed and gently pulled the pillow from under Masson's head. He spread his lips to welcome her, but seeing the gun so close to his head, he seemed to realise the danger, and no sound came from his mouth.

Alex's arm came down to the level of his genitals, placed the pillow on them, and inserted the barrel of her weapon.

The gun went off.

A howl ripped through the silence. Seized by convulsions, Masson threw himself on Alex and grabbed her wrist, in which he sank his teeth with all his strength, increased tenfold by the pain. Alex's reflex response was to drop her weapon and knock Masson down with her fist, throwing him to the ground where he rolled. Gasping and grunting, he began to crawl in fits and starts. His blood-slicked hands slid across the floor without finding a foothold. He wriggled his way to the far wall. His bloody crotch left a red trail on the floor like slug slime.

Alex recovered the pillow, her gun, and slowly approached. She was mesmerised by the blood dripping from the wound, genitals reduced to a pulp. The impact of the bullet had torn through everything from penis to anus; the trousers and flesh blown to shreds by the gunshot dangled in the air where, a few seconds earlier, there had still been genitals.

But as she aimed the barrel of her gun at the back of Masson's skull, she hesitated. No, she thought, not like that… and she kicked Masson in the ribs to force him onto his back. She stared at him and saw his lips move. He was addressing her. Was he asking for mercy? Her ears were ringing; she could hear nothing. Masson shook his head, his face emaciated and twisted with pain.

She got rid of the pillow and put her gun back on her belt. Masson's face relaxed a little despite the pain.

Alex unhooked the truncheon, held it in her hand, bent down towards Masson and delivered a first sharp blow to the jaw. This time she heard the dull thud of the baton as it hit his teeth. They shattered and were swept away in a spray of blood. Alex felt a violent cramp radiate from her lower abdomen. Masson had fainted under the intensity of the pain and lay inert beneath her. She cocked her arm again and struck Masson's head a second time.

A blow to the left.

A blow to the right.

With the regularity of a metronome.

With each one, Alex got a spurt of blood in her face.

She only stopped when there was nothing left to hit, Masson's head reduced to mush.

Gone, his carnivorous smile. Gone, his sadistic look.

When she realised that her face was covered with blood and fragments of flesh, she spat, and then angrily wiped herself with the back of her sleeve.

Finally, she left the cell, closing the door on Masson's lifeless body without so much as a backward glance.

THE LAST BITE

38.

It is a long white sandy beach. It is a beautiful day: the sun is high in the very blue, very clear sky, as on a winter's day.

Alex takes comfort from the sound of the waves recurrently rolling in on her feet, then receding. Seagulls hover overhead and squawk.

She turns around, and behind her is Michel's car: his old red Citroën AX. He is sitting in the passenger seat and smiles at her.

Malik is in the back seat, holding his head in his hands. Alex is happy to see him there; he is out of the hospital. He is doing well.

On the driver's side is Giancarlo. The door is open, and he is standing immediately behind it. Unshaven, as usual. He is smoking. He is staring towards the end of the beach, his eyes squinting.

Alex follows his gaze, and that's when she sees it: a tiny shadowy figure in the sunlight, moving in their direction. She runs, her ponytail bouncing to the rhythm of her stride.

She runs towards Alex. Her image comes closer, and Alex cannot take her eyes off her. She knows who this girl is. She cannot see her face yet, but she knows who she is.

The girl reaches Alex, slows down, and stops in front of her. She is out of breath; she shields her eyes from the sunlight with her hand as a visor and turns to Alex. Then she looks at the car, bends down to see who is inside, straightens up and nods to Giancarlo, who ignores her and continues quietly dragging on his cigarette.

Alex stares at her and recognises herself. This young girl is her much younger self: the Alex from before. She scans the horizon, still holding her hand as a visor as if she is waiting for something. She shrugs her shoulders and hugs Alex. Taken by surprise, Alex remains stiff and then abandons herself totally in this embrace. She cries softly. The Alex from before steps aside, smiles at her one last time and starts running forward again.

Going away.

Suddenly the sun and the seagulls disappear, and everything becomes dark and silent.

Then Alex hears a distant rumble swelling on the horizon.

It's getting bigger and closer.

A wave. A tidal wave, getting bigger and bigger. Now several metres high. Alex follows it with her eyes; she is afraid. The water is black, full of mud. Alex is paralysed with fright, unable to move as the wave continues to approach.

The wave curves and grows as it rises again and again into the air before breaking abruptly over them.

Alex, Giancarlo, and the car are swallowed up, swept away in a whirlpool of mud.

39.

'She didn't beat around the bush!' exclaimed Docteur Saranches as she examined Paul Dracques' body, or at least what remained of it.

Paul Dracques had been shot at close range in three parts of his body: head, heart, and lower abdomen. Nothing but craters of flesh and bone was left.

Docteur Saranches and Giancarlo faced each other on either side of the autopsy table.

Docteur Saranches became aware that this autopsy had some special significance and looked surreptitiously at Giancarlo: with a dark face, dark eyes, a beard several days old and drooping shoulders, Capitaine Ranieri was a shadow of his former self. It moved her. He and Capitaine Ramblay were a team she enjoyed working with, despite the unique circumstances in which they met. She was surprised to learn that Capitaine Ramblay had been committed. From a purely professional standpoint, she had found her to be remarkably thorough and intelligent.

'Since the cause of death seems obvious to me, what exactly do you want to know?'

Giancarlo scratched his beard without taking his eyes

off the corpse that separated them, particularly its abdomen. As he started to speak, his voice stuck in his throat. He had to cough into his clenched fist before he managed to articulate a comprehensible sentence, his Italian accent more pronounced than ever.

'Capitaine Ramblay and I were thinking of… cannibalism… I'm looking for some proof.'

Docteur Saranches remained silent for a few seconds while staring at Giancarlo.

'The child was still intact,' she recalled.

'I know.'

'Did you have the freezer searched?'

Giancarlo nodded and explained: they had found nothing significant so far, no limbs, no human remains. Scant traces of blood had been taken from the freezer, but they would have to wait for the analysis results to know whether it was human or animal blood.

'What makes you think of anthropophagy?'

Giancarlo pouted, seemed to be searching for words and finally said: 'A hunch… The limbs still not found, the way the mutilations were done. Nothing specific…' he added, seeing Docteur Saranches' doubtful expression.

'For the record, I just said that the cuts were clean and methodical. It reminded me of a butcher. I wasn't implying…'

Giancarlo ended the conversation by shaking his head impatiently and pointing again to the corpse's abdomen with his chin.

Docteur Saranches grabbed the scalpel and opened it from the bottom up. She plunged her hands in and pulled out the stomach pouch with great dexterity.

'You realise that you won't have the answer right away?

First, the digestion would not have to be too far advanced. Secondly, I would have difficulty differentiating human from animal flesh with the naked eye,' she added, weighing the pouch and recording the organ's weight on her Dictaphone.

Giancarlo looked up and locked eyes with Docteur Saranches: 'I know all that. There might be another possibility… We had another suspect. I have the impression that we didn't get to the bottom of it. And unfortunately, he's not the one who'll be able to tell us more…' confessed Giancarlo, pointing to Paul Dracques' corpse.

Docteur Saranches' arm stopped dead in its tracks, her hand holding the liver suspended in the air.

'You think,' she said, 'that he wasn't the one who was eating them? He was someone else's butcher?'

Hearing this possibility stated aloud made her doubt again. They had no concrete proof, either of cannibalism or the vet's involvement. Only Alex's convictions pushed him to persevere along this path. And if he couldn't find anything tangible, he would have to close the case and keep his doubts and the bitter taste of unfinished business to himself.

Alex had killed not only the butcher and his accomplice but also the two protagonists who would have helped them understand the motive, support, or refute their hypotheses. When Alex pulled the trigger, she had shattered the only hope of concluding the investigation with any certainty. Twelve 9mm bullets had destroyed their chances of finding the answers to their questions, getting to the bottom of the investigation, tracing the instigator: the person who ordered the children from Paul Dracques and his wife.

Giancarlo closed his eyes to try to avoid the idea that if

Alex had not been wrong—and she had proved to him so many times that she had unparalleled flair—then the respite would only be short-lived.

And the child killings would soon resume.

40.

'We've just received the first analyses from the lab,' Malik announced, wincing in pain.

He straightened up on the sofa to shift his body weight and relieve his still throbbing left hip.

Giancarlo returned from the kitchen with a pack of beer. The coffee table was littered with photos and sheets of paper: some typed, some handwritten. The whole investigation spread out in a jumble before their eyes. They had fled the Bastion to find a little peace and tranquillity. The station had been in turmoil since recent events: Alex's execution of the criminal couple and her escape from Sainte-Anne.

Giancarlo pushed a pile of documents to make space at the corner of the table for the beers. Malik was watching him, wondering how he was doing when he slumped into one of the armchairs beside him.

'Have you heard anything?' asked Malik.

'From Alex? No, they have men posted outside her building, at Michel's, and here too.'

'I was thinking of your wife and children,' he said, scanning the empty flat.

Giancarlo looked down, grabbed a can of beer, and

opened it. The pressure in the can released with a slight hiss floated in the air. He brought it to his mouth, staring at the silky foam that had spilt slightly over the top, and before dipping his lips into it, replied laconically: 'They're at my mother-in-law's house.'

Malik lifted the fax from the lab and handed it to Giancarlo, summarising the main points: 'The blood found in the freezer is of animal origin. In the cellar, they found several different types of blood… more than fifteen. Compatibility searches are underway.'

Giancarlo grabbed the sheet, ran through it quickly and threw it onto the table.

'I don't know anymore,' he admitted.

'The garden excavations started this morning,' Malik continued.

He rearranged the papers, trying to see the case from another angle, to find something they had not already seen that would make it possible to confirm or discard the third man and cannibalism hypotheses. He was unconvinced. In his opinion, the story went no further than the two people she had executed. Admittedly, they would not have the opportunity to question them, to shed light on the origin of the abductions and crimes, to go back in time and clear up several disappearances that were potentially down to this macabre partnership. They would have to wait for the results of the excavations. But as far as Malik was concerned, the case was closed, and there was no longer any reason to worry. Coldly, he thought the work was done, and even if there were still grey areas after the latest investigations, the case had been solved. He was amid these reflections when there was a knock on the door.

Giancarlo and Malik exchanged circumspect glances,

both in a state of uncertainty, as if they were not sure they had heard right when there was another knock on the door, louder this time.

Giancarlo stood up and walked with heavy steps to the front door. He peered through the peephole, swore under his breath, and opened the door wide. He blocked the entrance with his broad stature.

'How did you get through? There are two men posted downstairs.'

In response, Alex shrugged her shoulders as if it did not matter.

'I've come to surrender, Giancarlo.'

He stared at her for a long time: her hair was dirty and rain-soaked, her complexion very pale, her cheeks emaciated, her lips dry. Her eyes were bloodshot, the sockets sunken. Her look expressed deep weariness. Yet, she was stood straight before him and held his gaze, indifferent, resigned to the consequences of her decision.

'Not today,' he replied and stepped out of the way to invite her in.

They had read and reread, gone over and over all the investigation elements into the middle of the night. And when they realised that they were going round in circles, they agreed to stop there and let the night do its work.

Malik refused to stay and had gone home. Giancarlo had slumped a little more in his armchair and fallen asleep. Abandoning Alex once more.

She watched him in the dark. She had understood that Giancarlo and Malik no longer believed in her. She had caught the glances exchanged surreptitiously; they had hurt her. Especially Giancarlo's, who seemed to be saying

'I don't recognise you anymore' every time he looked at her.

There was no mention of the latest events, neither her escape from Hôpital Sainte-Anne nor Masson's murder at Fleury-Mérogis. It was as if she had crossed a line that her friend could not come to terms with. A great feeling of solitude enveloped her like a heavy icy blanket that someone had laid over her shoulders.

She went to take a shower and stood under the scalding water until it was stripped from her skin. She wrapped herself in a towel when she got out and stood in front of the mirror above the sink. The humidity and heat had deposited a thick mist on the mirror, and Alex could barely make out her face. It was time to face reality. She rubbed the mirror with her clenched fist to remove the condensation and better examine her face.

Her hair was wet, curly locks clinging to her forehead; the barely healed gash cutting across it a reminder of the escape from Hôpital Sainte-Anne and its perimeter wall. Her eyes were bloodshot, her pupils dilated, her hollow cheeks reddened by the scalding water. Finally, she gazed at the scar at the corner of her mouth. She closed her eyes and leant against the edge of the washbasin until her knuckles turned white. He was dead. By her own hands. She let out a sob. In a rage, she straightened her head and once more faced her reflection and that scar around her mouth, which would forever imprint the memory of Masson.

'You belong to me now and forever. This mark is my seal,' he had said.

Life and death, she thought.

It was no use. No door could close on that past. No

psychotherapy could help overcome that trauma. And that night, she understood that revenge had not succeeded in doing it either.

It was always there.

On her.

Inside her.

He was right: she belonged to him.

She gagged, bent double over the sink, and spat out all the bile that had just gushed into her mouth from deep within. She stood up straight, gave herself one last uncompromising look, and then dried herself off in a hurry.

She had one last mission to accomplish.

She could not leave this world until she had rid it of another Masson, a man who devoured children to make them his own, to possess them.

Alex got dressed. She stepped out into the night which welcomed her with its wet arms, without a word, without a sound.

THE LAST BITE

41.

It was 4:00 a.m. Alex stood a few metres from the front door of the building where Docteur Hugot lived. Autumnal drizzle was falling on her and a sheet of mist lounged a little further up the boulevard. She leaned against the icy wall behind her and paid no attention to the smell of rancid piss coming from the lamppost beside her.

She hadn't moved a millimetre, nor had she noticed that the streetlight had gone out as day dawned.

The neighbourhood quietly began to come alive. Several dump trucks passed by; the newsstand opened its doors, ready for people starting to rush to the metro station down the street.

A few pigeons circled her, occasionally pecking the pavement with their beaks.

At about 6:00 a.m. she heard the door click at last. On the lookout, she turned her head to see who was leaving the building. A young woman carrying several coloured nylon shopping bags struggled to get out through the door. As she stepped onto the pavement, Alex slowly moved away from the wall and in a few strides was at the door before it closed completely. She slipped inside without anybody noticing her. But it did not matter anymore, not really.

Alex hesitated in front of the lift. Docteur Hugot lived on the fourth floor, and he was an athletic man. He could just as easily leave his house by the stairs while Alex was in the lift. It was still very early, and his office certainly wouldn't open until eight. Alex made up her mind quickly and went up the stairs three at a time. Barely out of breath, it was when she stood in front of his door that she pondered what strategy to adopt. She first put her ear to it. No sound. She stepped back and noticed the doors of neighbouring flats a few metres along the narrow corridor. It would be highly unusual to be disturbed by a zealous neighbour playing the hero if they heard suspicious noises next door.

She remembered the layout of the flat. Their last visit was only a few days old, but it seemed to her to be an eternity ago. It was as if time had dilated since then due to the force of recent events. Her stay at Sainte-Anne particularly, when she was doped with anxiolytics and other chemical additives that had only added to her mental imbalance. She had the feeling that this last visit belonged to "before". Before everything fell into… into what exactly? Madness? Hysteria? What was the nature of this torrent she had been caught in without realising? Despite herself, she wanted to say, but she knew deep down that she was lying to herself. She was the origin, the power, the destructive waves. Not to mention that Giancarlo had abandoned her. He had taken his eyes off her, left her alone in that car. And everything had gone wrong. It was as if holding back this impulse simmering inside her for so long had become unmanageable, required too much effort, too much suffering to contain. She had given up the fight. She had consented to let herself go wherever her heart dictated, which had pushed her to the edge of her limits and far beyond the boundaries of the law.

Alex pushed away these ideas that continually tormented her, flayed her from within and turned into acidic doubts perforating her mind to prevent her from acting again.

In trying too hard to protect the innocent, the law had once again sided with the guilty, as is often the case.

No, they had no proof.

Yes, her intuition, her *flic*'s nose was probably seriously impaired.

But she felt it, there in the pit of her stomach. How could she explain it to Giancarlo and Malik, who no longer wanted to hear it?

It was him.

She knew it.

She had only removed one link in the chain. More kidnappings and murders would follow. Once he had reorganised himself, rebuilt his network.

More children, more victims.

And this was intolerable for him.

Alex would have liked to smash the door down and go straight in, but the door was armoured. She had to wait a little longer. She leaned against the corridor wall, closed her eyes, and breathed slowly, deliberately. She had to clear her head again. Silence the noises of her soul for a few moments more. Concentrate on her goal.

When she heard the chain rattle.

She opened her eyes.

She was ready.

The lock came undone.

And finally, the door opened.

Alex grabbed her SIG Sauer and stepped to the side to face the door. With all her might, she kicked the door handle. The door swung open violently, sending Docteur Hugot flying back against the wall inside the flat and shattering his nose with the sound of a broken branch, followed by a long scream of pain.

Alex walked quickly through the doorway to find Docteur Hugot sitting on the floor, his long legs bent, wedged behind the open door. He was half stunned, holding his bloody nose with both hands. She took care to close the door gently, which freed Docteur Hugot's legs, and he could slide them out on either side of Alex.

When he looked at her with a bewildered expression, he recognised her immediately. She was with the Italian policeman who had come to question him at his home a few days earlier and who had returned with a big black police officer just after the death of his receptionist and her husband.

'I didn't do anything… She was just my receptionist…' he murmured, nodding his head.

He coughed, embarrassed by the blood that was also running down his throat.

'I swear to you, I had nothing to do with this…' he continued, trying to hold Alex's gaze.

But the pain radiating from his head was too much, and Alex's gaze was as hard as steel. He gave up and closed his eyes with a groan.

Alex then placed the barrel of her gun on Docteur Hugot's forehead beaded with drops of sweat, and he began to sob.

She adjusted the barrel for the deepest possible impact

and fired.

THE LAST BITE

42.

Alex breathed deeply, absorbed in contemplating Docteur Hugot's face, exploded into a thousand spatters of blood, bone, and brain, on the wall and on her face.

She was decidedly getting too close to death these days.

She didn't even bother to clean up her face to remove the slimy, hot body matter.

She stepped back, felt her legs give way under her and stumbled into the living room to sit on the sofa in front of the bay window. Elbows resting on her knees, she looked up and watched the building opposite's windows light up one by one.

The day was beginning for some, and her day would end here.

She heard police sirens stretching out in a distant echo in the early morning.

She looked down at her SIG Sauer, scrutinising every detail as if she were discovering it for the first time: black with a slender grooved barrel that she knew inside out and handled instinctively, it had extended her arm and hand so well for so many years. Strangely, at that very moment, it felt heavier in her hand.

She slumped against the back of the sofa, letting her arms hang down her body. Her eye was drawn to the wrist in which Masson had sunk his teeth one last time before he died. Her wrist was smooth and intact. She looked at her other arm: no trace. She rolled up her sleeves and stroked her skin from the crook of her neck to her wrist, trying to recall the moment he had bitten her after she fired at his crotch. Then she decided that Masson would not be in her thoughts at such a singular moment, and she firmly chased this final recollection away.

She slowly raised her arm and pushed the still-warm gun into the back of her mouth, compressing her tongue and scraping her palate. She held back from swallowing as she felt the bitter taste of gunpowder stinging her throat and eyes.

Finally, she asked herself who would look after Michel in her absence and pulled the trigger.

Epilogue

'Capitaine Ranieri?'

'It is indeed.'

'Officer Reno here. I'm calling because we found what you were looking for at the bottom of the Dracques' garden.'

'*Aspetta*[44],' Giancarlo interrupted immediately, 'wait for a second,' he resumed.

Immersed in reading the preliminary report from the forensic police on the evidence taken from Paul Dracques' vehicle, Malik instinctively raised his head. Giancarlo waved to him, and he stood up with his usual nonchalance, accentuated since being beaten up by the Pyramides gang.

Giancarlo removed his glasses, massaging the bridge of his nose lightly, then squinted to get a better look at his mobile's digital keyboard. He pressed the speaker icon and held out his hand.

'Continue.'

'We have probed the garden in several places, and at

44 *Wait up*

the back of the house, in the septic tank... *No! Don't touch anything else and leave it to me now! ...* Sorry for the interruption. The medical examiner has just arrived. Anyway, we found a lot of... *Get out of the way, get out of the way, for heaven's sake! We need to protect them from the rain immediately! ...* arms, legs, in a bad state, rotting,' he said, coughing. 'I'm not surprised he put them in there!'

    '...'

    'Capitaine, can you hear me? ... *Is it Ranieri? Put him on!* ... The pathologist wants to talk to you...'

    'Ranieri! I just had a quick look. From what I could see, the limbs would match the age of the victims. On the other hand, despite the putrefaction... *Oh, how it stinks, it's worse than the smell of the dead...* I don't think any of the flesh was removed. The limbs were not... how can I put it... cut into. I'm afraid your anthropophagy hypothesis does not hold water.'

    '...'

    'Ranieri? Are you still there?'

Printed in Great Britain
by Amazon